HEARTLESS

MICHAELA WRIGHT

For the man whose name I do not yet know.

ACKNOWLEDGMENTS

I must thank the Algonquian, Ute, and Lakota people, as their history and stories heavily influenced this book. They've heavily influenced much of my life.

Gotta thank the historians who poured over the Alfred Packer story, plucking out details that helped influence this book.

And thank you to my mother, who forcibly dragged me through the Old West part of the country on road trips with my grandmother. I learned how to entertain myself through some of the most palpable boredom you can imagine, but I also absorbed a lot of history. So thanks, mom. We didn't need to stop to take seventeen pictures of that monument, but thank you, nonetheless.

CHAPTER ONE

SHE COULDN'T FEEL THE feather on her calloused hand. That is, if he's even touching me yet, she thought.

"Do you feel it at all then, girlie?"

Cadence frowned, her hair plastered to her forehead beneath the blindfold. She shook her head.

He chuckled, her hand shaking in his before he let go. "See, told ya. Now just imagine how weightless such a bird is."

Cadence pulled the blindfold up over her head, squinting to settle her sights on the saloon around her. She gave a shake of her head, letting her blonde hair cascade down her back. Maxwell tucked the hummingbird feather back into his pocket and gave her a smile. She'd grown to like Maxwell since he first began performing in the evenings at her saloon. He wasn't as popular with the regulars as the burlesque girls, that was sure, but he was a good respite from hiked skirts and thrown change.

At least, she thought so.

There was a loud thud over by the bar, and she shot a glance to her stepfather, Calvin Hoover, who stood glaring behind the bar wiping down a glass. Without a word, she understood his meaning – quit entertaining the entertainment and sell some god damn booze.

Cadence smiled at Maxwell, the friendly traveling magician. "You'll have to tell me how ya managed to catch the little fella one of these days."

Maxwell smiled. "Oh, it were easier than you'd think! See, Hummingbirds love -"

"Maxwell, God damn it! Let the girl work, will ya?"

Both Cadence and Maxwell started to hear Calvin hollering from behind the bar. Maxwell gave her a resigned shrug, smirking as he did. Cadence patted him on the shoulder and let him return to his bag of tricks, setting up for the show.

The Red Onion saloon wasn't the nicest watering hole in town, nor was it the cleanest, or the friendliest, but despite Calvin's demeanor, it was the busiest by a country mile – and it was hers. And it was just as her Pa and Mama had imagined it – save for those damn burlesque girls. It wasn't a cesspool where you'd need to be deloused after leaving, but it could get rowdy, especially after a rousing show of ankles and knees.

That was the word to describe the Red Onion – rowdy. Cadence often watched local miners and railroad workers get hammered to their heart's content, only to lose their minds on each other after an unfortunate round of poker.

Don't play if you can't win, Cadence thought. And definitely, don't play if you can't lose.

Not many men agreed with that outlook.

"Alright, honey. What's a man gotta do around here to get a god damn drink?"

Cadence turned to meet the gaze of an older gentleman settled at one of the half empty poker tables. "Well, for one, you gotta say please, now don't ya?"

The other men at his table burst into laughter, but the man's thick mustache seemed to go even straighter as he glared at her. He wasn't a miner or a railway worker; this man clearly had a few dollars in his pocket. Interestingly enough, he wasn't the only man of means to prefer the Red Onion. Perhaps the burlesque ladies could take credit for that. They were among the best in Cheyenne. They hiked their skirts up just a bit higher, so Cadence was told.

Cadence sauntered toward his table, her head held high as one of his fellow card players shuffled the deck.

"I'm lookin for a refill, here. The other idiot woman still ain't topped me off."

The man's hair was slicked down, parted in the middle, and his vest was still buttoned up tight, though his jacket hung over the back of his chair. He had a small monocle chain hanging from his vest pocket, and his mustache was trimmed so straight, she was sure he could level a floorboard with it. Cadence knew him well – Cecil Tennant. Cecil stank of banker from his pomade to his leather shoes and the small wad of crisp notes on the table before him only assured further. Still, just like the rest of the men at the table, his shirt sleeves were rolled up to the elbow.

It was common knowledge in the Red Onion that even bankers could be cheaters – or more aptly, the bankers were the worst kind.

"Well, what was she bringin you? I'll see if I can't fetch it for ya."

A sudden burst of sound toward the stage announced Maxwell's show was about to begin, and Cadence leaned in to catch the man's drink order.

She almost didn't hear the word 'bourbon' as the door to the saloon swung open, distracting her from her business.

She wasn't the only one to notice the shift in the air, as the saloon took on a strange lull for but an instant.

The man standing in the doorway stood with his coat tails swung back, showing a lack of weapon at his belt. He felt armed, nonetheless. He was clad in black from head to toe, looking more like an undertaker than a saloon patron. His hair was a dark, dusty brown, and he had severe features; sharp, well-bred, with a jawline that went for days.

Cadence wasn't the only one staring at the man as he sauntered into the saloon heading to the bar. Even Maxwell's magic show had taken a back seat to the sudden fixation.

When men like that came into the saloon, they usually brought bad news, or they came looking for bad news – outlaws or bounty hunters in search of outlaws. Yet, this dark man simply took a lean on the bar, whispering his order to Calvin before turning a disinterested eye to the rest of the room.

That disinterest seemed to release everyone from their spell, and the piano player picked up his usual jaunty tune.

"Alright, I'll get that bourbon for ya," Cadence said, giving Cecil a tolerant nod.

He shook free of the same spell as she spoke, his eyes darting toward the bar in discomfort. Cadence couldn't help but wonder what trouble a banker might have with this kind of man.

"Dolores is being useless again, Cal. Tennet ain't got his bourbon for god knows how long."

Calvin shot her a sideways glance, still pouring the order of the man in black. She set her tray on the bar and waited a moment before storming behind the bar herself and grabbing the bottle.

"Hello, Duchess."

The voice sent a shudder through every inch of her. She didn't have to turn around to see who'd spoken.

"Might I trouble you for a pull on that, myself?"

Cadence swallowed, only half glancing over her shoulder. The man in black's voice was deeper than any man she'd ever heard, and rough, like being dragged over rocks. She took down a second glass, only then realizing that Calvin had disappeared into the back room. Cadence poured the two glasses of bourbon and turned to face the man. He met her gaze and the feel of it nearly knocked her down.

She straightened.

He ain't done nothing to scare you. Don't be letting this man think he's rattled you just by calling you Duchess.

Duchess. She'd never heard any man call a woman such a thing. She turned around, setting the bourbon on the bar next to a shot of whiskey, letting the contents jostle almost enough to spill over. "So, where ya from, then?" She asked.

He set his long fingers on the rim of the glass and ran a fingertip along the perimeter. "Oh, a long way away."

He let every word ring, rolling over them like a sleepy dog.

"I gather you ain't from around here." She said, her chest puffed up in compensation of the strange tension she felt in his company.

He took up the first glass, swirled it around under his nose, and then shot her a look over the rim of the glass. “No, madam. I am not.”

With that, he leaned his head back and emptied the glass in one go. Then he set it back on the bar, snatched up the other, and soon set the second empty glass on the bar with a clank. Then without a word, he tapped his index finger on the first glass. She retrieved the bottle of bourbon and refilled it.

Calvin reappeared behind the bar, his energy as excited as hers. Yet, unlike her, Calvin couldn’t hide his nervousness. He set a wad of notes on the counter, and the man in black took it up in a graceful gesture, took his fresh glass of bourbon, and turned back toward the room.

Cadence watched the man saunter past the full tables, drawing curious and nervous glances from everyone he passed until he reached an empty seat. Then he settled into his chair, tossed a couple notes into the pot, and leaned back to wait for the round to finish.

“Who the hell is that?” Cadence asked, hissing at Calvin as he fidgeted behind the bar.

Calvin just shook his head. “Ain’t got a clue. Certainly, in a different mood than before, though.”

“What’s that?”

Calvin’s eyebrows shot up, and he leaned in. “He were in here earlier stirring up all sortsa ruckus.”

“When? I didn’t see any such thing!”

“It were mid-day, darling. Before you came down to work.”

Cadence turned toward the crowd, finding the stranger’s head and watching the relaxed posture he’d taken in his chair, sneaking a peek at his cards as the round began.

“How do you mean? How was he acting?”

Calvin gave an exasperated sign. "Never you mind, girl. Get back to serving up those drinks. Fella knocked the wind right outta the place. Need to perk everyone back up!"

She took a few drink orders, catching a wave from a regular here and there, and knowing their usual drink, procuring it without needing to ask. Despite the stingy nature of miners, Cadence never had want of tips from her usual crowd.

Cadence was back at the bar a few moments later and found Calvin staring across the tavern, seemingly transfixed by the air itself.

"Cal? Cal!"

He startled, turning to meet her gaze as though he'd thought himself alone in the massive space. "What the hell's gotten into you? Pour a girl a drink!"

Calvin shook off his momentary strangeness and delivered two glasses of whiskey. She watched him for another moment as he tried to busy himself by the register. Finally, she snatched up her tray and made her way through the tables as Maxwell earned his first heckle from the crowd.

"Show us yer tits!"

Maxwell gave a nervous laugh from the stage, ignoring the comment as other patrons laughed and joined in. Cadence turned to find the culprit, a dusty looking man who clearly spent much of his time underground, and she bore a hole through him with her eyes. His brown beard was blackened with soot, and his teeth glistened in shades of yellow and cream from within the brambles of his beard. He was too busy laughing with his pals to notice her watching him, so Cadence set down the glasses at their intended table, and sauntered up behind the man, before turning toward the stage. She gave Maxwell a quick wave, then Cadence held her arms out to her sides in a grand flourish.

Maxwell regained his composure on the stage and leaned over his top hat.

"Feast your eyes, ladies and gentlemen!" He called.

Maxwell waved his hands over the hat, and a second later, opened them to reveal a pair of white doves that quickly flew from his grasp, flying across the room. The crowd oohed and aahed as the white creatures flitted overhead, then as she knew they would, they homed in on her waiting arms, diving down to take up perch on her hands.

As the crowd gave a few half interested claps, she took a bow, holding one of her hands directly over the heckler's head. Then she dropped her hand just inches, causing the bird to tense as it held on. The tension caused the bird to loose its bowels, spraying a rocket of creamy white onto the soot covered head of the heckler.

The tavern exploded with laughter; laughter so intense some patrons could be heard spitting, pounding their tables, and in one case, coughing and hacking to catch their breath. Cadence stepped aside quickly as the miner demanded a rag from the other barmaid, Dolores, to clean himself up.

Cadence lifted her hands up toward the stage, and the birds took flight, returning to Maxwell who was busy fighting to hide his grin from the laughing crowd.

Cadence turned back toward the tables.

"What are you laughin at ya Cherry Ni-?"

The last word was drowned out by laughter, but Cadence knew what he said. She'd heard the phrase many times, and she knew instantly who the bird shit recipient was hollering at.

The Native man stiffened by the bar, fighting to hide his mirth as the entire saloon glanced toward the object of bird shit head's chagrin.

This man was wearing a suit, and his bowler hat was settled on the bar beside him as he leaned in to order his first drink. Cadence had served the fellow twice before and knew he went by the name White Foot. Cal was wiping the bar down in front of the man but froze to hear someone calling the innocent bystander out.

Cadence spun around on bird shit head. "What's your name, fella?"

He glowered at her, his head almost wiped clean. "Grant, why?"

"Why, Grant? Well, because Grant, we gotta rule in the Red Onion that ornery folk such as yourself ain't too welcome. So, to curtail your visitin further, your drinks now cost double! You have a nice evenin."

She spun back to snatch up her tray as the saloon burst into another round of laughter and teasing. Grant hollered his disdain, but there was little he could do at that point. She had spoken, and there wasn't a barmaid there that would go against her wishes. She caught White Foot's eye as she sashayed down the row of tables. He lifted his drink and gave just a hint of a nod. Cadence let her eyes speak for her.

A table of regulars – miners from the coal train who left sooty fingerprints on everything they touched – gave her a round of applause as she squeezed past them. She went about her business, a satisfied smile pulling at her own cheeks. She caught sight of a pair of dark eyes trained on her, and her smile disappeared.

The gunpowder voiced man in black was watching her, a smirk curling at the corner of his thin lips.

Cadence swallowed. Goodness, what was it about him that rattled her so?

She tried to avert her eyes from the man, squeezing between a couple tables as Maxwell requested one of the scantily clad burlesque girls, a redhead named Charlotte, be his volunteer. There was a round of hooting and hollering as Charlotte sashayed her way up onto the stage. Cadence grabbed a tray from the bar and began collecting up glasses and spent bottles. Another round of hooting betrayed Charlotte's willingness to show a bit of knee up on the stage, and Cadence rolled her eyes. However frisky Charlotte was now, Cadence knew Charlotte was a good Christian girl, saving herself for marriage despite her choice of employment.

A strange warmth started Cadence around just as a man's hand slipped up between her legs. She squeezed her thighs together, shrieking as she spun to find a greasy haired man with yellow teeth grinning up at her as his equally greasy hand pressed upward further. She scrambled to still his groping, but he only pushed further, the sweat and grime of his fingers easily moving upward. If she didn't grow stronger in the next two seconds, he'd have his hand in her pantaloons. Cadence grabbed his wrist in one hand, and as panic gave way to rage, she snatched up one of the empty bottles from the table and smashed it over the grimy man's head.

The whole saloon exploded around her, patrons and burlesque dancers alike all clapping and cheering as the greasy man slumped out of his chair toward the floor, his hand now settled squarely on his sore head. Her thighs felt grimy in the wake of his touch.

Cadence glanced around her, taking a deep breath to still her nerves. This was turning out to be one hell of a Tuesday night at the Red Onion.

"Cady! What the hell you doin out there?!" Calvin hollered as he rounded the end of the bar, coming to stand at her side, kneeling down to placate her assailant. "Hey there, Harry. She didn't mean nothing by it. I'll get the next round, shall I?"

"The hell you will! Get outta my damn saloon, you filthy bastard! If I ever see your face in -"

"Cadence Delacouer!" Calvin hissed.

She stopped, fuming so deeply, she was sure steam was rising from her ears.

The drunken, greasy man shook his head, rubbing his fingers into the stringy tendrils around his crown; blond hair that was so unwashed, it was turning brown at the root.

The yellow-toothed man nodded up, shooting Cadence an offended glare. "You're lucky we ain't alone, bitch."

"You ever lay a hand on me again, and you'll be pulling back a stump. You hear me, you son of a bitch?"

Calvin grabbed her by the arm, yanking her away from Greasy Harry as the crowd booed. Calvin shoved her behind the bar, pushing her into the back room and out of sight.

"You tryin to cost me money?" He said, pointing a finger so close to her face, she could have bitten it off.

Cadence set her jaw. She wouldn't be reprimanded for this. "I ain't one of your dancing girls; I won't tolerate no man treatin me like that!"

Calvin shook her, pointing the finger at her face again. "You ain't one of my dancing girls, but you sure as hell ain't here to cost me money. Can't very well sell the man a drink if he's afraid of getting beaned with the god damn bottle."

"He put his hand up my skirt!"

"Then let him!" Calvin hissed, accidentally spitting in her face as he did. "I don't need this from you, girl. I lose enough money having you here, as it is."

Cadence glared at him, her nostrils flaring. She knew well what he meant. They'd had this very conversation many times. "I ain't dancing the burlesque."

"You know how much money I lose having you here instead of another dancer? How much I lose every damn night?"

"*You* don't lose nothing! I know those fellas; I know their drinks. *We* make double what we'd make with another burlesque girl serving drinks, because I refill em before they even know they're done, instead of squatting in their damn laps and trying to pull side business in the back alley!"

Calvin's eyes went wide for a moment. The Red Onion was not a brothel, it was a saloon with entertainment. That didn't stop a good number of the girls offering up special favors to some of the most generous patrons. It was clear by Calvin's expression that he hadn't realized she knew he was keeping such a side business.

He took a deep breath, exhaling out his nose. "Would it kill ya so much to hike your skirt up from time to time? Show a little stocking, that's all them girls do."

"If you ask me again, I'll go down the bank and show them the deed."

Calvin's mouth opened, but he didn't speak. He didn't dare test this threat. He wouldn't test it because it wasn't his name on the deed, and it never would be. Cadence was the legal owner of the Red Onion saloon, just as her mother had wanted, just as her Pa had wanted before that.

"I let you play boss with me, but don't you ever get comfortable thinkin you're in charge of me. Never!"

Cal swallowed, glancing out into the tavern as the crowd clapped politely for Maxwell's final trick. "Fine. Here."

Calvin reached into his pocket and pulled out a wad of notes, pressing them into her hand.

"What the hell is this?"

Calvin jutted his chin toward the quieting room. "Table in the corner's clearing out. I want you to go throw in."

She glared at him. "God damn it, Cal. Now I'm playin cards tonight?"

"You complaining? I can think of several other girls out there who'd love to play cards at work."

Cadence followed his gaze and saw the table he intended her to play at. She licked her lips, her stomach turning over as she glanced at the empty seat to the right of the gunpowder voiced man. Could she refuse this? Would he slap her for it?

"Come on, girl. You're sharp as hell at cards. That table loses another player, and that'll be the end of that. Keep em here a while longer, will ya?"

Cadence looked down at the coins and notes in her hand and snorted. She closed her eyes tight a moment, clutching the crumpled paper. Then she marched out into the tavern, rounding the bar with such determination that the greasy haired man flinched at the sight of her approach.

Good, she thought.

"You fellas mind if a lady cuts in next round?"

There were three men seated at the table, but there were five chairs, and Cadence stood just behind the one beside the man in black. Cecil Tennet was still there, his sleeves still rolled, his hair still primly parted down the middle. Yet, his brow seemed heavier now, just as his pot seemed lighter.

He puffed at his cigar, giving her a skeptical look before waggling his eyebrows at his fellow players. "I don't know, boys. Do we have room?"

The gray-haired mining foreman scoffed, but didn't speak, straightening up to make room for her to sit down. The man in black shot her a sideways glance, gesturing almost surreptitiously with those long fingers of his.

The gesture seemed to say in bemused indifference, 'Why not?'

Cadence tossed a penny into the pot as a gesture of comradery and gratitude, an old-fashioned habit Calvin taught her when he first married her mother, Frances. She was only twelve at the time. Well over a decade and a half later, she still had the same habit.

Cadence watched the three men play, twirling a strand of blonde hair in her fingers. She let the first two hands go by without much fuss. She was biding her time, watching intently. By the third round, she'd noticed patterns. Tennet's lips went white when he had a good hand, a sign he was pinching them between his teeth. The mining foreman rocked his jaw when his cards weren't any good, betrayed just slightly by the twitching of a pair of unruly hairs just under his left ear. If the hairs were moving, he was gonna lose.

The man in black was a harder nut to crack. He was leaned into the arm of his chair, his coat hanging out around him as he tapped his cards, almost indifferent to the rest of the room. His flat-brimmed hat was still settled squarely on his dark head, and he barely said a word as the three men went around, giving up their cards and waiting for the fates to shine a little brighter.

The foreman's beard hairs went still; he'd gotten what he wanted from the deal.

The man in black didn't move at all.

The banker's lips had returned to a healthy shade of pink.

"Read em and weep, boys!" Said the miner, fanning his cards out onto the table to show them his three aces. Cecil exhaled, tossing his cards out to show a pair of kings before snatching up his glass and draining the last of its contents.

Well done, foreman. Take that banker for everything he's worth, she thought.

"Hang on there, fella. I might have something to say about that."

The man in black set his cards down on the table with a dramatic and slow flourish. Full house.

The foreman slumped back into his chair, slamming a hand on the table as the man in black leaned in to collect the pot, pulling it toward him with a satisfied grin.

He gave a nod to the banker. "Well then, Cecil. Are you going to deal our new friend in, then?"

Cadence watched the banker's hands as he shuffled, making a point to catch his fingers and the placement of his hands on the table. It didn't look like the man was cheating. In fact, she wondered if he'd have survived this long if he was prone to such endeavors. Anyone with a keen eye could read the man's face like a cloudy day.

Suddenly, the stranger turned toward her, offering a straight-toothed smile. "So, my dear. Might I ask your name?"

Cadence fought not to show what the man in black's attention did to her nerves.

Come on, girl. We're playing cards. Poker face.

"Cadence."

The man in black's eyebrows shot up. "Well, isn't that an unusual name. I've never met a woman named Cadence before."

"That's because it's a man's name," the foreman grumbled, picking up his cards with a grimace.

"I've heard that it's fast becoming a popular girl's name as well."

The foreman gave her a skeptical look, raising an eyebrow before snorting softly.

"Perhaps it suits you," the man in black said. "You strike me as rather musical, in one way or another."

"Tell that to anyone that's ever heard me sing," she said.

The man in black chuckled, and he seemed almost startled by it.

"And you are?" She asked.

Both the other men at the table perked up at this. The man in black clearly knew Cecil's name – Cecil Myrtle Tennet was more than happy to spread his name through town – yet it seemed his fellow card players hadn't learned his. They waited, watching him. She wasn't the only one he made wary, it seemed.

"You might find this interesting, but my name is Shannon, actually."

The foreman openly laughed at this. "Well, your Pa must've had a sense of humor. Get beat on as a kid?"

Shannon shook his head. "Interestingly enough, no. Most boys know not to cross me."

The air instantly left the room.

Cadence swallowed searching for words to fill the silence and break the spell. "Shannon? Well, I guess we've got something in common," she said, casting a steely-eyed look at the cards in her hand.

Shannon turned his attention to her and smiled, leaning into the table to collect his cards, and the four of them settled into their first round.

Cadence watched each of them; the jostling beard hair, the white lips. Still, Shannon betrayed no signs as he played the next two rounds, winning both. Cadence made a point to fold both times, giving an exaggerated sigh as she did.

Finally, the third round came, and Cadence looked down at the worst hand she'd been dealt thus far – a pair of twos. She smiled.

"Alright, boys? Are we in, then?" Shannon asked, brushing his coattail back behind him as he settled his elbows on the table. The foreman threw in, as did Cecil. Shannon turned to watch her, raising an eyebrow in wait of her decision.

She threw in as well. Both Cecil and the foreman stiffened to see it.

Play it off, girl. You've got the best hand in the house. Play it right.

Shannon stared at her, as though examining every inch of her face. She felt almost challenged by this.

You want to see through the cracks, you son of a gun?

She was going to make him work for it.

Cadence stared at her cards a moment as the betting opened with Shannon. He upped the ante by two bits.

She nodded, smiling at her cards. Then she fought to straighten her face as she matched Shannon's bet. "So, Shannon. Where you from?"

He raised an eyebrow, setting two cards down on the table to trade with the dealer – the foreman this time. "Why do you ask?"

She shrugged. "Well, because of the way you talk."

"What about it?"

She shrugged, tapping her cards on the table. "You don't sound like any fella I've met. Sound almost fancy, but you dress like a god damn hangman, so I'm just curious."

Cecil's eyes went wide, but he didn't dare look at her.

Shannon smirked. "Fancy, you say?"

"Yes. I'm guessing you're from Eastward somewhere? Maybe Chicago. Or further?"

Shannon licked his lips, flicking the corner of one of his cards as he leaned back in his chair.

The foreman gave Cadence her two cards.

Damn, she thought as she pulled the six and the seven. Still the worst hand in the house.

"I'm from Boston, actually."

Shannon called on his turn to bet, turning it to her. All three men turned to watch her. She feigned oblivion to their impatience. "Boston, huh? Do they all talk fancy up in Boston?"

Shannon shot her a sideways glance. "I imagine some must."

"Come on, girlie. You gonna play, let's play," the foreman grumbled, glaring at her.

"Oh! I'm sorry!" She said, grabbing another two bits and throwing it in the pot.

The foreman sighed, tossing his cards down as he folded, followed by Cecil.

Shannon turned his attention back to her. "My turn to ask a question."

Cadence's eyebrows shot up, but she watched him lick his lips as he flicked the corner of his card again and leaned back. "That fellow over there – the one with the unfortunate encounter with a dove -"

"Yes, I know the one you mean," she said, fighting not to let her brow furrow.

"Did you do that on purpose?"

Cadence tried to force her face slack. "I certainly did."

He licked his lips again and nodded. "I thought so."

They both sat there a moment, watching each other. He took a deep breath, flicking the corner of his card. She waited for the familiar gesture. A moment later, he licked his lips again.

She snorted softly. "I think you're just trying to distract me from the game."

He feigned shock. "I'd never. I'm just curious about you. Any woman who can smash a bottle over a brute's head like that is worthy of notice."

The saloon doors opened again, and Cadence shot a quick glance toward the door. The man in the doorway had short hair, the bushiest mass of hair across his upper lip, and the look of the dead about him. She watched him a moment. She'd seen the man in the saloon once or twice before, but never paid him any mind.

Now, he stood there as pallid as a corpse, hovering like some vampire that needed inviting in. She was about to shoot Calvin a wave to alert him to the strange behavior when Shannon tipped his hat toward the door. The man with the bushy mustache turned and disappeared out into the night, as though running from his own shadow.

Cadence turned to look at Shannon. He seemed as disinterested as though a fly had come through the door.

He must be a bounty hunter, she thought. Still, if that was the case and this mustached man was a bounty, why hadn't Shannon gone after him? Surely his hand wasn't *that* good.

She tapped her cards on the table. "Fella had it coming. And worse."

Shannon leaned onto the arm of his chair, his voice taking on an even deeper resonance that seemed to almost hum in her chest. "I have no doubt."

"I think a girl like you should mind her place, if you ask me," the foreman said, irritated and impatient with the growing comfort of his company's conversation.

"Well, thank goodness no one asked you," Shannon said, deflecting the man's insult with a set brow. Despite the apprehension this man caused her, she felt somehow giddy to think he'd taken offense on her behalf. "Are you raising, Duchess?"

Cadence straightened in her seat, determined to break his spell. Duchess – that word didn't help her in the slightest.

She tossed another two bits into the pot.

"Are you touched, girl? Jesus, it's like playing with a god damn imbecile."

Shannon licked his lips, flicked the corner of his cards, and smiled across the table at Cecil. "Watch your tone, Mr. Tennet."

Cadence bristled to hear Shannon defend her again.

Come on girl, she thought. You can damn well do it yourself.

"Is it?" She asked. "Well, ain't that grand coming from a fella who can't keep a poker face to save his damn life."

Cecil straightened, but she continued.

"Mr. Tight Lips. How have you ever won a hand with that face of yours?"

The foreman got a satisfied grin at this. She was sure he wasn't the only laborer in the place who'd like to see a banker set into.

She glared at the foreman. "Don't get too jolly, you. You give yourself away just as bad."

The foreman looked down at himself with the sudden embarrassment of a man with his fly down.

Shannon chuckled. "You're never going to find another man willing to play with you if you give away all of your secrets, dear."

She turned on Shannon, dead set against letting him rattle her further. "Well, why not? I know you got a shitty hand right now, and you're trying really hard to decide whether or not to press me. Let me guess, a pair of twos?"

Shannon's face didn't change at all, but his eyes grew darker, the black at their centers dilating as he watched her face.

She held her breath. Her desire to be brave had only made him more intimidating.

Had she awakened a dragon? Would he retaliate to this wise talk with anger, disdain? Would he curse her with that somehow musical voice of his – a voice one would expect to break through the skies on judgment day?

With achingly slow speed, the corner of his mouth began to creep upward. He took a deep breath, exhaling through his nose. "Well then, little lady. I fold."

Cadence watched him set his cards down and fought not to smile. The man was holding a pair of sevens.

She felt his power over her relent just so, and she smiled. "Well, that's a shame. I thought you had me read."

Cadence set her cards down, face up, and the foreman exploded, swearing at her with a complete lack of concern for propriety. "You halfwit whore! You don't even know how to play the game! Pair of God damned twos?!"

Shannon's eyes darted toward the gray-haired man, but he didn't speak. Cadence just leaned over the table, snatching up the large pot and pouring it over into her lap. "Well, if that's how you're going to speak to me, I'm guessin you don't want a chance to win any of this back. Y'all have a nice night."

"No! God damn it!" The foreman roared as she scooped up the coins and notes in her skirts and made her way across the tavern. She was happy to be free of the game – happy to stop pretending to be less intelligent than she was. And despite the strange discomfort Shannon brought her, she was almost disappointed to leave his company. Strange to find something so frightening and alluring all at once.

Cadence dumped her skirts onto the bar as several patrons began to notice the foreman's complaints – and her triumph – calling out to her their approval as she began to count her winnings. She had friends among the Red Onion's patrons, and the foreman wasn't the most popular man amongst the other miners, it seemed. Still, before Cadence could shoot a mischievous grin to her cheering section, Calvin appeared on the other side of the bar.

"Thought I told you to keep em playin. Don't think I mentioned emptying their pockets."

Cadence rolled her eyes. "You want me to play cards, I'm gonna play cards. I let em win two rounds before I took em."

Calvin shook his head as he wiped down the bar. "Did you give yourself away?"

Cadence frowned. She had.

Damn it, why did she do that? To impress Shannon? She cringed to admit it.

"As long as those two idiots ain't in here, I can play again."

"Sure, ya can," Calvin said, glaring at her before he spun around to put away glasses.

The evening began to wind down, and just the regulars with eyes on winning back their losses or on spending time with one of the burlesque girls remained. Cadence went back to clearing tables and topping off drinks, keeping an eye on the man in black. He and the two other men continued to play for a few more rounds before Cecil gathered up his coat and headed out for the night. The foreman remained for another two or three rounds, finally rising to leave in a huff well past midnight. Cadence made her way behind the bar, dropping a handful of coins into the jar by the whiskey bottles – her night's tips. Sad to think a woman who could claim ownership of a tavern had to relish in the collection of tips each night. At least Calvin wouldn't demand a cut anymore as he did when she first started working in the saloon.

Calvin rang a bell behind the bar, announcing the last call to the stragglers that remained. Only two of the half dozen men required refills.

She pulled up her sleeves behind the bar, hoisting up the water basin onto her hip. "I'm gonna toss this out back and head upstairs. Are you alright with that?"

Calvin nodded, his attention fixed on giving the register a quick gander.

She sighed and turned toward the back door. The hallway was dark in the back of the saloon, and the alley was even more so as she stepped outside into the damp air. The night had been gray, and drizzling rain brought a good crowd in for a mid-week night. The moisture in the air seemed to seep through her dress, prickling at her skin as though someone stood behind her. She stepped down the alley to the end of the building and tossed the basin of murky water out into the mud.

"I'd say you owe me an apology."

Cadence dropped the basin, turning toward the sound of the voice with a shriek.

The foreman stood in the shadows, his crooked teeth the only visible part of him.

"I don't owe you a damn thing," she said, fighting to keep her voice from wavering. She didn't have a bottle to smash over this fella's head.

"Oh, I do believe you do. An apology, and I'd say about three dollars. I'll take double that for my trouble, though. I'm sure you've got that and then some in that little jar of yours."

The foreman stepped toward her, coming into the light just enough for her to see the shiny metal pick in his right hand.

She swallowed hard. "You're a god damn coward, you know that? Coming after a woman in the dark like this? I ain't giving you a dime, you son of a -"

The foreman stepped forward, grabbing a massive clump of her blonde hair, and pulling her toward him so she could feel the sharp edge of the pick pressed to her ribs. "Don't test me girl, or I might do worse than just cut you."

His breath smelled of bourbon, onion, and rot as he yanked her back down the alley.

"Now, we're gonna head on inside, grab what's rightfully mine, and you're gonna deliver it to me real calm like."

"You don't know me, you dirty prick."

He chuckled in her ear. "Oh, I will soon enough if you don't watch that mouth of yours."

"All I gotta do is scream, or tell Cal -"

"I wouldn't do that. I might have to hurt him, too."

She jostled against his hold, but all it did was pull strands of her hair free. She flinched as he tightened his grip. "Girl. I know where you work. I know where you live. I have friends all over this town; men who work for me every damn day. Some of those bastards ain't so nice as me. Guess what they'll do if I give em the order to make you hurt? I promise you, honey, you won't be no Duchess when they're done with you."

She felt squeamish instantly but didn't speak as he pushed her toward the door.

"Now, you gonna be a good whore and get what I want, or am I gonna have to send nice fellas to come convince you?"

"These fellas don't sound so nice to me."

The foreman started around so roughly, Cadence felt more of her hair pull free. They turned to meet the source of the voice.

Cadence stared at the unfamiliar man, waiting for the next shoe to drop. His skin was darker than hers, and his hair was long and black, but his face was almost completely obscured by the wide brim of his hat. The Native man stood a good six inches taller than the foreman, and he leaned into the wall of the building with such an air of disinterest that she almost questioned whether he'd spoken at all.

Then the terrified side of her muttered her silent fears – was this man one of the 'friends' the foreman warned her of.

"Mind your own god damn business," the foreman growled into the dark.

Despite the close proximity of the voice, the Indian man was almost invisible in the alley. The foreman pulled her back, and she stared wide-eyed and pleading into the dark.

"I suggest you let the young lady go, sir," the native man said, lifting his head just enough to show dark eyes beneath the brim of his hat.

The voice had changed, dropping to a deeper, rougher place. She felt her legs begin to tremble beneath her. Though the voice didn't threaten her, the immensity of the man's presence was enough to leave her shaking. This was the second time in one night that a man took the air from the place.

"I'm just here for what's mine. You run along to whatever hell hole spawned you," the foreman said, pushing the pick further into her side. She was sure her dress was tearing from it.

The hand yanked at her hair, pulling her head back with such force, she almost toppled to the ground. A second later, the hand was gone, and the full weight of the foreman's body dropped to the ground behind her, toppling into her legs as he did. She stepped away, fighting to catch her balance as the foreman rolled into her. Cadence felt the figure beside her before she could make out the shape of him.

"Are you alright?"

Her legs nearly gave way beneath her, and she fell toward the wall of the saloon. The native lunged toward her, holding out an arm for her to steady herself. The notion of touching this man made her pull her hands away from him, as though she'd been caught touching some holy relic. Her breath began to come in heaving bursts, and her vision grew bright at the edges.

"Breathe slowly. You're alright."

"Don't you tell me what to do!" She hissed, fighting to steady herself.

She wasn't alright. Though the foreman was lying still on the ground, the presence of this stranger beside her was immense, overwhelming, as though she stared up at a thundercloud that reached miles into the sky. She pushed her hands in his direction, willing him away. Yet he did not retreat, taking hold of her and walking her toward the door of the saloon. "Come now, girl. You go back inside."

She met his gaze and for the first time, did not shirk from it. This man towered over her by several inches, and his eyes were so dark, they seemed black. Yet there was a warmth to his expression, and for a moment, his mere presence didn't cause her knees to shake.

She took a moment, letting her breath settle. "I'm sorry I was short with you."

The native smiled. "You don't owe me an apology. I'm no more than a strange man in an alley to you."

"Ain't that the truth," she said, stumbling like a drunk at last call. "Still, you sure ain't the fella that was poking me in the ribs."

"That I'm not. I assure you, he will pay for his beha -"

"Why? What you gonna do?" She asked, unsure whether the thought of the foremen meeting an unfortunate outcome soothed, excited, or scared her.

The stranger gave her a skeptical look. "Do you want to know out of concern for the man, or your own satisfaction?"

She frowned, turning her eyes away from in an attempt to storm off. Her legs had other ideas, and a moment later she was careening into the clapboard of the saloon's wall. The man appeared at her shoulder, offering his arm. Cadence moved along with him as though propelled by an unseen force, her mind barely capable of putting one foot in front of the other.

Had she almost just died?

Had this stranger not come, would she be alone and bleeding in the alley, or would men have come to find her some other day and hurt her?

Would they still when this protector was gone?

Cadence fought to settle her mind, letting the stranger hold her about the shoulders as he led her into the back rooms of the saloon. The air was thick with whiskey fumes from old barrels, and she found herself swaying in the wake of it. The man pushed her forward gently, urging her to move along with him. As they reached the end of the hallway, Calvin glanced back at them both, shooting her an annoyed, quizzical look.

She pulled from the stranger's grasp.

"We gotta call the sheriff down here. I ain't letting that fella get away with this. He don't know who he's dealin -"

"It will all be taken care of. You need to settle your mind, sit down for a moment. Come on."

"No! I'm fine!" She swatted his hands away. She couldn't stand the idea of Calvin seeing her being 'handled' like this. "Who the hell are you to be coddlin me?"

He cracked a smile, betraying a full set of clean, white teeth. "Your blood is up. You need to -"

"Don't you tell me what I need!" She said sternly, marching past him toward the main room. There would still be stragglers left among the tables, and Persephone would still be courting her miner for extra attention. Cadence considered what Persephone would find if she took her customer out back tonight. Cadence steadied herself to charge forward. Persephone needed to be warned about the unfortunate scene. That is if the foreman didn't regain consciousness and come barreling inside to finish his errand.

And Cadence had chores still to complete.

She had a saloon to run.

She had things to do.

Don't be weak, she thought. Don't you let them see you weak.

Cadence slumped into the wall again. Her heart was racing, and she could hear her blood pulsing in her ears.

"God damn it," she mumbled to herself. She didn't like needing someone, but she was in shock. She'd heard stories from other girls – burlesque dancers who'd been roughed up and worse.

Cadence had been lucky. No man had dared to do more than sneak a hand up her skirt. After all, her stepfather was the proprietor of the place. Still, Calvin hadn't been too protective recently, a symptom of his frustration. Maybe he'd show a little concern if she just hiked her skirt up.

She swallowed as Persephone caught sight of her barely upright in the hallway door. Persephone came rushing over just as Cadence turned to thank the native man for his help. Sadly, when Cadence opened her mouth, it wasn't 'thank you' that came out. "And what the hell were you doin out there in the first place?"

But the man was gone, and Persephone rushed into the empty hallway glancing around for whoever Cadence was talking to. When Persephone found the hallway empty, she gave Cadence a worried look. Persephone's fretting had begun.

"You alright, hon? You look like you've seen a ghost."

Cadence glanced out into the saloon and found Shannon gone as well. She stood there a long moment, feeling the sting of the shiny metal pick's damage in her side.

"I'm fine, Seph. Damn it!" Cadence said, her tone growing angry as Persephone continued to fret. "Just – will ya just help me upstairs?"

"Of course," Persephone said, wrapping an arm around Cadence.

"Stop, don't make it look like I'm hurtin, alright. Just act natural – for once in your life."

Persephone laughed at this and sashayed her way around the banister with Cadence in tow, leading the way up the stairs.

Cadence stumbled up the steps, and once they were safely nestled into her room, she told Persephone what had happened.

Cadence wanted to call the Sheriff down, wanted to see the foreman in irons, but her better sense told her such dreams were no more than smoke on a windy day.

Persephone could vouch for the Sheriff office's unfortunate history. Women getting roughed up in alleys wasn't exactly their biggest concern.

"I just don't want him – or any of his friends comin back."

Persephone glanced out the bedroom window, craning to see down into the alley. "I don't see anybody down there. D'ye think your new friend dragged him off, maybe?"

Cadence shook her head. What reason would the native man have of managing her problems? She wasn't the first woman to be threatened in that alley, and she probably wouldn't be the last. Surely the native man simply set off to wherever it was he was heading in the first place.

"Cady? Where the hell are you, girl?" Calvin called from the bar downstairs.

Persephone rose for her perch on the side of Cadence's bed and opened the bedroom door for Cadence to holler back.

Before Cadence could draw the breath to yell, Persephone smiled at her, raising a hand. "I'll handle him. You rest, alright? Get some sleep."

She made to protest, but she'd lost whatever fight she had in her for the evening. Cadence slumped back into her pillows and listened to the sound of her heart slowing.

It had certainly been one eventful night. Cadence sat there a long moment, replaying the moments in the alley, her stomach tightening. She fought to push the thoughts aside, remembering instead the look on the bastard's face when she took him at cards. The memory was bittersweet. She enjoyed knowing she'd outsmarted him, but his warning was haunting her.

Was it only a matter of time before he – or worse, half his friends, returned to do her harm?

She sat up in bed, leaning into the window to look down into the alley. The pane of glass reflected half her face in the light of her bedside lamp. Cadence turned the lamp down until the room was full dark, then leaned into the window again for another look. Motion at the far end of the alley caught her eye and shot her heart into her throat. An instant later, recognition struck as the native man pulled the wide brimmed hat from his head and offered her a gentlemanly bow.

Then in the silence of the city at night, the stranger turned up the main road and disappeared from sight.

CHAPTER TWO

A WEEK PASSED WITH no sign of the mining foreman or his 'friends.' Cadence still took extra care, refusing to venture into the back alley on her own. Calvin grumbled his disapproval to cart the water basins out himself, but he knew better than to argue with her once her mind was made up. Cadence didn't bother to tell Calvin what happened with the foreman. He wasn't much of a man of action, and she didn't imagine he'd be all that sympathetic to her troubles. The foreman was business, and business was all Calvin cared about.

There was one other detail of the foreman's absence that tugged on her mind.

She found herself glancing out into the busy streets looking for a familiar face.

Two familiar faces.

She didn't spot Shannon or the native man anywhere.

Cadence scolded herself for thinking about the smoky man that appeared in her hour of need. He'd never ventured into her saloon before that night, and there was no reason to think he would now. Still, she couldn't help thinking about him from time to time.

Jesus, Cadence. Stop being such a ninny, she thought. He wasn't the first man to ever show her kindness. Besides, he was native. There was no chance she could ever be with a native man. Her stepfather would kill her, and that's after some angry mob killed him.

Then there was Shannon – flirtatious, well-mannered Shannon.

He'd given her the eyes more than once, and unlike the native man, Cadence could be seen with him were she to let him woo her.

Let him woo you, Cadence. Would you listen to your damn self?

Cadence distracted herself with busy work, pushing any lustful thoughts for either man from mind. She wasn't ignorant to the finer points of men. In fact, she'd lain with a man before, and it was enough of a disappointment to turn her into a nun. Still, something about the way the stranger made her feel - safe, maybe. The confidence and the mischief of his demeanor even as she behaved like a green broke filly. That kindness made her think of him often. That and the worry the foreman was due to return any day.

Damn it, Cadence. Native. Indian. A red man – stop thinking about him. Think about Shannon. Shannon is fine.

Damn it, no! Don't think about him either. Think about washing this damn glass!

She would never admit it, but she'd sat at her window each night looking for a sign of the native man tipping his hat up to her window.

"Wake up, girl! We got deliveries!"

Cadence jumped, nearly knocking a glass off the bar. Calvin had caught her staring off into space, twiddling the ends of a rag in her fingers. She'd been daydreaming about the man in the alley again, and the dark eyes that seemed to bore right into her.

Foolish girl.

"Don't you yell at me, Calvin Hoover. I'll get to it when I damn well get to it."

Calvin rolled his eyes at her, but she snatched up her shawl and headed for the door. It was a short walk down the main roadway to the Post Office, but she resented being bossed around no less. Cadence bust out the front door of the saloon, letting the outer doors swing back and slam shut behind her. Calvin hollered his disapproval from inside.

Cadence bounded down the steps, careful not to trudge through the mud of the dirt road. Cheyenne was growing in population with every day, many prospectors still making their way west with their heart set on gold. First, they'd come on their way to California, then they were heading up toward Alaska – anywhere a loud mouthed man might steer them, the gold-hungry would follow. She'd seen livelihoods made and ruined in search of gold. Some men fell for a tall tale, buying up land to mine only to find the hillside harbored little more than squirrel shit. Others struck it rich but lost it all at the tables or to thieves. She felt sorry for these types. They carried a sadness to their eyes that only comes from having tasted happiness, then lost it. Still, even they had something to be thankful for – they were still alive. There were a good number of prospectors who couldn't say the same.

"Cadence!"

She turned toward the light voice and found Persephone running up behind her. Persephone had long, dark hair, and her skin was dusky and warm. Cadence smiled to greet the burlesque dancer, her hair curled up under a cap like a proper lady now that she was out in the daytime.

"Morning, dearie," Persephone said, hooking arms with Cadence. They sauntered down the wood planked walkway toward the bank and post office.

"Have you heard the exciting news?"

Cadence shot Persephone a sideways look. "No? I ain't a gossip. You know that."

"Oh, that's right. I forgot."

They walked another ten feet before Cadence shook her arm. "Alright then, tell me!"

Persephone got a mischievous grin. "You'll never guess who they've found hiding out in town!"

Cadence's eyebrows shot up. "Who?"

"Alfred Packer," Persephone said, whispering as though his name might offend a passerby.

Cadence gave her a skeptical look. "Good grief. I ain't got no idea who that is. Here I thought you were gonna say Buffalo Bill, or that Billy the Kid was still alive or something."

"You don't know who he is?" She asked, shock driving her pitch up by three octaves.

Cadence rolled her eyes and took off walking again.

"Lord girl! Will you listen? Ain't you remember them stories everyone was telling a few years back? Bout that prospecting bunch that went up into the mountains and never came back down?"

"Which one?" Cadence asked, sarcastically.

"The one where one of em ate all his friends."

Cadence stopped in her tracks and turned to look at Persephone. "He did what?"

"Turned cannibal. Murdered his friends and ate em. Came down from the mountains after months looking all bright-eyed and bushy tailed – and well fed."

Cadence touched her hand to her stomach, feeling queasy. "Stop, Sephy. You're makin me ill."

"Well, he's here! Heard they's bringing him to jail, right now."

"Maybe you should go stand with all the looky lous and watch it as it happens."

Persephone put a hand on her hip. "You know, maybe I should. Not that an angry mob ever looked poorly on a girl like me in their midst or anything."

Cadence took a deep breath. She'd witnessed the unfortunate comments that Persephone received. It seemed many didn't take too kindly to a woman like Sephy anywhere but in a cotton field. "I'm not going with you, Seph."

"Come on! It'll be a story to tell your grandkids!"

"No. I got errands to run, thank you very much."

Persephone rolled her eyes. "Fine. 'Spose I shouldn't be surprised."

"No. You shouldn't."

"They been lookin for him for nigh on ten years, Charlotte says."

Charlotte was another burlesque dancer, and well known for her flair for gossip. There wasn't a man that crossed Charlotte's path that didn't part with his secrets – a fact Charlotte had suffered for more than once, with a black eye and a broken nose.

"I'm sure Charlotte would go with you to ogle the cannibal."

"She's already there! Come on! Just imagine the bounty that fella musta had on his head."

Cadence stopped, staring down at the wooden planks before her as a carriage trudged by through two inches of mud.

Cadence had never gotten around to asking whether Shannon was a bounty man or not, but perhaps that was what brought him into town. Perhaps he'd be there.

Hell, if it was as big an event as Persephone was making it out to be, maybe they'd both be there.

God, Cadence. You're a silly girl. Stop it.

"I know you want to," Persephone said.

Her wavering resolve was playing on Cadence's face, it seemed.

Cadence took a deep breath. "Fine. I'll go have a look, but I ain't stayin all afternoon. Some of us have to work for our tips."

"Oh pish," Persephone said with a smirk, hooking her arm with Cadence's before setting off toward the Sheriff's office.

The crowd was gathered around the jail, many of them ranchers and miners, as well as the more well-to-do of Cheyenne. A woman in a wide-brimmed hat and mink shawl gave Persephone a long glare. Cadence shot the woman in the mink stole a sideways look.

Prim and proper to all her friends, but down the jail to catch a glimpse of the cannibal.

Miss Mink Shawl and Persephone weren't so different after all, Cadence thought. She silently relished the look such a declaration might get from the high and mighty woman just as the crowd began to hum and jostle around them.

Something was happening down toward the street – the wagon was pulling up.

"Oh, Lord. Here he comes. Cady, I'm all a flutter. Are you nervous? I'm *so* nervous!"

Cadence stood on her tiptoes, still trying to pretend she wasn't curious. Yet, she wasn't searching for a sight of the cannibal Parker; she was looking for familiar faces.

"Monster!" Someone called within the crowd.

That was it. The whole spectacle was in an uproar. People jostling each other to catch a glimpse, hollering their insults, some even throwing trash toward the center of the crowd as the prisoner was pushed toward the jail. "Can you see him? Damn it, I'ma knock this lady's hat off her damn head," Persephone hissed, being careful not to be heard. Persephone may have been a free woman, but she knew well that freedom had stipulations. One of those stipulations was not acting too free.

The crowd shifted backward, knocking them both back a couple steps. Cadence moved away from the crowd, climbing up a small incline in the roadside to catch a better look. She scanned over the sea of faces and saw the prisoner being led through the angry crowd.

Cadence's mouth fell open. "Oh, my goodness! I know him!"

The prisoner's shoulders came up with each violent outburst, but she saw his face clearly – there was no mistaking that mustache.

"You what? No, you don't, girl. You lie!" Persephone said, scampering up the incline to join Cadence.

She caught a glimpse of the bushy mustache just as a bunch of the crowd saw their ideal spot and shoved them aside to take a look.

Persephone had a thrilled expression that quickly faded to disgusted shivers. "Dear Lord, I may well'a sat in that maneater's lap!"

Cadence ignored her friend, charging down into the muddy street to catch the best glimpse she could of the crowd. She remembered the look on Alfred Packer's face when he saw Shannon. Did they know each other? And if they did, surely Shannon would be here. Cadence scanned the crowd, searching for the familiar dark hat, hoping she might find him by his mere presence. The crowd heaved and swayed as Alfred Packer was led up the front steps. Suddenly, the man surged to the side, as though trying to get away from something. Alfred's eyes were trained toward the far end of the crowd, and his face took on that same ghostlike shade it had in the Red Onion. Cadence moved fast, rounding the edge of the crowd to set eyes on whatever it was Alfred saw.

"He's here! Damn it, he's here, fellas!" Alfred said, shifting in the lawmen's arms.

Cadence hurried past the crowd, scanning the road ahead. A figure moved across the road, his posture strange and unsteady, as though he too ran from something.

"Shannon!" She called.

The running man seemed deaf to her calls. She tried again, louder this time. "Shannon! Shannon!!"

He stopped by the third call and turned toward her. They stood there a long moment, him staring her down as though she'd shown him the fear of God. It was Shannon, but he seemed strange. She put out a hand, walking through the street toward him, but his light eyes looked right through her. Then, he turned down the road and ran, his feet kicking up puddles as he disappeared around the corner.

She watched him go, feeling a sudden tension in her belly. She stared down the bustling street for a long moment as though hoping he would reappear. Finally, she turned back toward the crowd, searching for her friend.

The intent gaze of a stranger startled her to her surroundings. Her breath stilled in her chest as she met the dark gaze. The native stood just a few yards away, his face inches above many, his long black hair hanging loosely over the shoulders of his dingy gray coat. He wore a wide-brimmed hat over his head, shielding his face from whatever sunlight the cloudy sky might offer. Yet even under the shadow of that hat, his dark eyes burned into her, as though he inspected every flinch and movement.

Like a hunter watching a nervous deer.

She furrowed her brow, straightening up to speak to him. "I didn't get a chance to say, 'Thank you,'," she said, but the words were barely audible even to her. Something about his presence nearly knocked the wind out of her, and in the light of day, it wasn't just the intensity of his gaze.

This man was one of the most beautiful people she'd ever seen.

He smirked from beneath the brim of his hat, then turned toward the road and headed off. He'd disappeared from view before Cadence realized he'd followed the very same path as Shannon.

Cadence stood there a long while, letting the excited crowd jostle around her.

"Well, Lordie. I'm gonna sleep better knowing that fella is locked away."

Persephone was still regaling her by the time they rounded the last corner to the Red Onion. "I'm sure," Cadence said, barely listening.

"One of my customers last night was tellin me all about the murderin bastard. Said he up and killed his party with an ax."

Cadence shook her head. She didn't want to hear anything more about the man they called The Colorado Cannibal. She had other things on her mind.

Both Shannon and the native man were there. Knowing they were still in town, but hadn't come back to the saloon – not even for a game or a drink? It made her frown.

"I was readin in the paper this morning that Packer claims it wasn't him that killed everyone. Says it were another man went crazy in the mountains, murdered everyone while Alfred was out hunting or some convenient nonsense."

"Mmhmm," Cadence said, pushing the saloon doors open with her hip as Persephone followed her inside. Persephone stopped just inside the door and shot Calvin a friendly nod.

"Afternoon, Sheila," Calvin said.

Persephone coughed softly, and Calvin recovered.

"I'm sorry. I mean, Persephone."

"Good afternoon to you as well, Cal."

Persephone shot Cadence a wink and set off to the back rooms, giving a few men a quick touch on the shoulder as she passed. Though Sheila was the name Persephone grew up with, when Cal successfully convinced her to take her job as a barmaid to the natural conclusion of burlesque dancing, Sheila had chosen a different name – a stage name, she called it.

'All the serious performers have one,' she'd said. 'Something a bit more mysterious. No fellas gonna find Sheila Rheinhorn mysterious.'

Cadence rounded the bar to check in with Cal. There were early patrons throughout the saloon, but the room was dim in the late afternoon, Calvin not having lit the torches yet for the evening.

"Where you been off to?" Cal asked as he poured the contents of a cheap whiskey into the now half empty bottle of pricier drink. Charge twice as much if you're willing to sneak a little swill in with each pour of the good stuff, he'd said the first time she noticed him doing it. Cadence didn't like the practice, but it was his place to run, technically. And a little swindling on the whiskey wouldn't bring the bank crashing down on them.

"Was down by the jail. They brought in a shady character. Persephone dragged me down to catch a look at him."

"Was it everything you'd hoped it would be?" Calvin asked, shoving the stopper into the top of the now full bottle.

"Given I weren't expecting it to be nothing at all, I'd say it sure was."

Calvin chuckled. "Well, I'm expecting a bit of a crowd tonight, as per usual."

They could always expect a crowd in the public houses whenever anything of note happened in town. By tomorrow, every Tom, Dick, and Harry would know what Alfred Packer had for dinner.

Calvin stared into the rows of glasses. "Did you see him?"

Cadence pulled her apron down from the hook, tying it at her back as she nodded. "I did."

"What'd he look like?"

Cadence stopped, the knot only half tied. She hadn't considered Alfred much since catching sight of him, but now that Cal asked, she remembered the startled look in the man's eyes when he stood in the door of the saloon nights before. He seemed a frightened sort of man, not the heartless, cold-blooded eater of men that so many would have her believe. She opened her mouth to speak but thought better of it. She imagined her description would only disappoint him.

And they said women were the sex that liked to gossip.

"Like any other man," she said finally.

Calvin shuddered dramatically, then eyed the room's patrons. "Makes you wonder."

Calvin was starting in on combining another bottle of cheap whiskey when Cadence sauntered out into the main room to check on her regulars' drinks. She was happy with the distraction.

The evening crowd was more than doubled that night, evidence of the excitement down by the jail. Cadence heard conversations, all boisterous and overlapping each other until they all but combined. Persephone was the evening's darling, several tables paying out the nose to have her come over and describe the surly bastard now festering in the Cheyenne jail.

Cadence refilled drinks, listening intently to the tales as they grew more outlandish with each passing hour.

"Is it true he had caked blood in his mustache, Sephy dear?" Martin Leed asked in a slurred drawl. Martin was a former miner who'd made a good stake out west, earning years' worth of a living in one month. He'd come home to Cheyenne in a nice suit and hat a year earlier and was happily drinking away his prospects ever since.

Cadence shot Persephone a sideways glance, but Persephone didn't see it. "Oh, that and God knows what else?" She exclaimed for everyone to hear.

Cadence rolled her eyes. "Come on, now," she mumbled, slipping between a usual pair of carousing buffoons who for the first time in months, paid her ass no mind as she passed. Their attention was wholly on Persephone, and anyone else who had a detail or two to share about the cannibal, Alfred Packer.

"Jesus, we're out of Wild Turkey." Calvin stared up at the mirrored wall, his lips pressed together beneath his handlebar mustache.

Cadence set her heavy tray onto the bar and rounded to join her stepfather. Without a word, she ducked down to a cabinet beneath the bar, tugging a fresh bottle of the stuff from beneath.

"What in the hell is that doin down there?"

Cadence wiggled an eyebrow at him. "I had a feeling tonight would be rowdy. Here ya go? Should taste the same as the last bottle."

"What's that s'posed to mean?"

"They're both a tiny bit watered down. Made three bottles turn into five."

"You brilliant girl! No wonder your Ma left ya the place."

Cadence smiled wide at this.

"Might I get a glass of the not so watered down stuff? I'm happy to pay a bit more."

Calvin and Cadence turned to face the source of the voice. Calvin began stumbling over his words to respond, but Cadence didn't even try to speak.

Shannon's gaze had returned to that same soul rendering intensity, despite the jovial smile on his face.

Calvin coughed. "I'm sorry, sir. I'm sure she were just jokin around."

"No need to apologize, Mr. Hoover. It's business. A man needs to keep his roof, even when the locusts try to eat him out of house and home."

With this Shannon gestured toward the crowd.

Cadence swallowed as Calvin produced a bottle from the back room, pouring Shannon a tall glass of their finest bourbon.

"On the house," Cal said, giving Shannon a meaningful and pleading look.

Shannon shook his head and set two bits on the bar. "I'm not strapped for cash, friend. I'm happy to pay. And I'm happy to keep this all between us – that is, if you'll allow me to steal your lovely daughter for a time."

"Of course!" Calvin said with a tinge too much excitement.

Shannon shot her a sideways look as he raised his glass to Calvin. Shannon turned from the bar and offered his elbow to Cadence.

"You think I'm something you can just order from the bar, then?" She said.

He held his elbow to her without a word, taking a sip of his bourbon as he waited.

She exhaled out her nose in frustration, but she took his arm. "Ain't gonna have a quiet moment. We only got two girls on the floor tonight. These are some thirsty fellas."

"I can only imagine. Still, I have a thirst that needs slaking as well and unlike the rest, only you will do."

These words sent shivers through her that made her hands squeeze his arm just a bit tighter. He noticed, glancing down at her fingers. Shannon led her across the saloon, pulling a chair out for her from an empty table – a table he'd clearly laid claim to upon entering. Apparently, she wasn't the only one who found him intimidating.

She took her seat, her hands fidgeting in her lap as he took a seat across from her. "How have you fared these past few days, then?"

"I've been just grand. Thank you."

"I'm glad to hear it. I'm sorry I had to leave without a goodbye last time we met. Something came up -"

"Oh, it's fine. You did miss a bit of drama, though."

"Oh? Do tell."

Cadence took a quick moment to share the frightening events in the Red Onion's back alley. Shannon's face grew concerned as she spoke. "I do hope you haven't seen any further from this surly fellow."

"No. Ain't seen him since. And how about you? How've you fared?" She blurted, a tone of accusation in her voice. Though he'd apologized for leaving so abruptly before, he'd run from her in the street. Run as though she were chasing him with a hacksaw.

His brows shot up over his bourbon as he stifled mid-sip. "Why I've been just grand as well."

"You didn't seem all that grand today."

He stopped, setting the bourbon down between them. "No, I imagine I did not."

"You on the run, then?"

"I am not."

"You sure about that?" She asked, her confidence building. Why was she being so forthright – and downright ornery with this man?

He smiled at her and she felt her resolve fading. "Did I upset you somehow, dear Cadence?"

She set her lips tight, but words came, nonetheless. "You sure ran at the sight of me today."

Shannon reached across the table and set his hand over hers. Her words stilled instantly as a searing sensation traveled up her arm from the warmth of his hand.

"Let me apologize, dear Cadence. I did not mean to upset you. Perhaps I was too distracted to realize you were there."

"You looked right at me. I called your name."

Shannon squeezed her hand and she tugged it away, not out of disdain for his touch, but out of nerves. His touch made her body respond against her will. She'd never felt anything like it. She shot him an apologetic look but did not speak.

"I am sorry, Duchess. I behaved unforgivably. Please do accept my apology."

She looked up to find his dark eyes softened. He seemed so different now than he had that afternoon. He'd gone from a man who looked more like a frightened animal to this regal creature before her. What on earth could have made him that afraid?

Was it Alfred Packer? Did he know something about Packer that the rest of them didn't?

"Hey, girly! I need another round!"

Cadence turned to wave off the customer – a bearded rancher she'd only seen once or twice in the previous year. Yet before she could speak, the rancher took one look at Shannon and blanched. "Do forgive me. Didn't mean to interrupt."

Cadence turned back to find Shannon shooting the man an almost jovial glare – jovial, but nonetheless foreboding. Even she felt inclined to recoil from it.

"Well then?" She asked, glancing nervously about the room. Despite having wanted this man's company for days, now that she sat with him in the rowdy saloon, she felt guilty to neglect her business in lieu of idle banter. "What'd ya want with me?"

Shannon grinned and it disarmed her completely. That grin felt almost filthy, even as his words were innocent. “I enjoy your company, m’lady. I was hopin you might enjoy mine as well.”

“To what end?”

“To whatever end ya like.”

She heard the innuendo and glared at him. “So, you think I’m just gonna bed ya because I pour drinks for a livin -”

He chuckled softly. “No, Duchess. If I bed you, it will be because you damn well wanted me to.”

She stifled an almost cry to hear him speak so brazenly. The cry embarrassed her, and she felt her cheeks grow hot.

She spun in her chair, ready to leave him just to save face. She didn’t want him to see how easily he could rattle her. “And here I thought you were a gentleman -”

“Do you want me to kiss you, Cadence?”

She stopped halfway out of her chair. She shot him a startled look, opened her mouth, but no words would come.

He smirked. “Thought so. Alright then. You get your pretty little backside back to work. I’ll be here when you’re done.”

Cadence launched herself from her chair, nearly slamming into a nearby table as she tried to put distance between herself and Shannon.

How dare he speak so barefaced? Did he think her less of a lady simply because she made her wages in a saloon? Then beyond these thoughts, her stomach knotted into itself with each step. Did he mean it? Would he wait all night for her?

Then what?

Cadence rounded the bar and slipped into the darkness of the back room, pressing her back to the wall as she caught her breath.

Dear God, he affected her.

She pressed her hand to her chest, feeling the thrum of her heart within, and waited for it to slow.

"Ya done pussy footin around then, girl? Got drinks to serve!"

Calvin stuck his head through the dark doorway, giving her a quick once over before his brow furrowed. Then he turned back toward the bar, hollering his chagrin as he went. It took her another three minutes to get up the nerve to step back out into the saloon – and into view of the man with the gunpowder voice.

The crowds didn't start clearing until well past midnight. Calvin had to hit the last call bell three separate times to make sure everyone heard. Still, they lingered in the saloon for another hour past last call, and all the while, Shannon remained in the corner of the saloon, almost taunting her with the slow sips of his pricey bourbon.

"Well that bastard looks mighty pleased with himself," Calvin said under his breath when Shannon was one of the last three patrons still loitering within the Red Onion. Cadence fought to hide her nerves from Calvin as well as Shannon.

Persephone gave a late night 'Whoop!' to let everyone know she'd had a damn fine night in tips. Even Maxwell was in a good mood. Apparently, gossip hounds enjoyed magic shows.

Calvin was washing down the bar as the last couple miners stumbled out the swinging front doors.

"We're closing up for the night there, friend," Calvin said, letting his voice resonate across the room as though he was too polite to directly tell Shannon to get out.

Cadence knew her stepfather. He didn't suffer from politeness. She was sure Calvin's caution was due to the same reason she had hardly made her way through the far corners of the room since Shannon first arrived. Something about him felt unnerving – captivating, but dangerous.

Only more so now that Cadence suspected he was on the run from the law.

What man in the Red Onion wasn't? She thought.

"Will you take care of whatever it is he wants, already?" Calvin hissed under his breath.

Cadence shot him a glare, setting the heavy tray on the bar. "What makes you think he's here for me-?"

The sound of chair legs grinding against the floor startled her around, and she found Shannon rising from his seat, pulling his coat from the back of the chair.

Was he really leaving? Had she done something? Had she taken too long?

What are you on about, Cadence? Ya haven't so much as shot him a glance in nigh on three hours! Course he's had enough!

Cadence took a few steps across the saloon floor toward Shannon but could not bring herself to speak.

He smiled, pulling his coat on. "You have a good night now, dear."

Then Shannon turned for the swinging saloon doors and disappeared out into the darkness of Cheyenne's quiet night streets.

Cadence gave an exasperated sigh. All that nervous tension and her evening turned out to be a bowl full of nothing.

This felt just about as insulting as Shannon running away that afternoon – perhaps more. The man was beginning to confuse the ever-loving hell out of her.

Cadence directed her frustration at her friends. "Alright, you lot. I got chores for ya if you're just gonna lounge around."

Persephone groaned from the stage, the other three burlesque girls having cleared out with customers. Maxwell shot Cadence a smile and rolled up his sleeves, making his way around the room, flipping chairs onto tables so Persephone could sweep.

Calvin gave a whistle from behind the bar. "You! Come round and take this out back."

Cadence glared at Calvin, eyeing the wash basin with disdain. She hadn't done this job since the night the angry foreman cornered her in the alley. Her side still showed the mark from his pick. She wasn't in a hurry to start the chore up again. Still, Calvin had let her off without so much as a grumble for days. There'd been no sign of the foreman since. Still, the thought made her nervous.

That would matter little to Calvin though, and she knew it.

It was her saloon after all.

She took a deep breath and hoisted the heavy basin up onto her hip, the murky water sloshing up at her as she sauntered past the stage and out toward the back door.

The floorboards creaked just a little louder in the back side of the saloon, a symptom of years of shifting foundation beneath. She set the basin down long enough to swing the back door open and stopped, listening to the quiet remnants of activity as the drunks teetered home down Cheyenne's dark streets. A hoot in the distance betrayed a rancher mounting his horse with a bit more gumption than was necessary. The sound of a horse neighing angrily, followed by the sound of a surly bastard crashing to the ground made her chuckle. What a sight that must've been, she thought. She stepped out into the dark alley and could hear others laughing in the distance with her. Cadence smiled the whole way down the back alley. She reached the back street and tipped the basin over to drain down the hillside and away.

The angry rancher was bellowing on in the distance, something about the horse being as stubborn as his wife, and further laughter echoed across the distant streets. She joined the chorus of laughing voices, unafraid of her volume. Another laughing voice joined her, far closer than the rest.

She spun around to see a dark shape leaning against the wall of the Red Onion, clad from head to toe in black. She was sure he'd been there when she came out of the saloon, but he faded into the shadows as though he belonged there.

"You tryin to give me a god damn heart attack!?" She hissed. "I damn well told you what happened before!"

Shannon struck a match and held the flame to the end of a wooden pipe. The familiar smell of tobacco wafted through the alley toward her. The smoke was a far more pleasant smell than the alley was often home to.

"I do apologize, Duchess."

Cadence wiped her hands against her apron, feeling nervous and exposed. "You got an affection for brooding in dark alleys, then?" She asked, doing her best to give each word bite.

He puffed on his pipe again and the orange light illuminated his face a moment, letting her meet his dark eyes. "No, I can't say it's the alley that I bare affection for."

Cadence tensed. Her heart had almost leaped at these words.

What a foolish girl you are, she thought. *Getting all giddy over some carousing gambler who comes breezing through town with a kind word.*

"Sure, ya say that to all the girls."

He smirked. "Can't say that I do."

She swallowed. She wanted very much to believe him, but her better sense was sternly shaking her head somewhere. "Well, can't say I'm all that flattered by compliments only paid in dark alleys."

"I'll pay you a compliment anywhere you like."

Shannon took another two puffs on his pipe, then tapped the contents out into his palm and brushed them on his pants. He tucked the pipe into his coat pocket and turned to her. "I'm afraid my kiss will taste of tobacco now."

Her eyes went wide and her mouth fell open.

He grinned. She hoisted the empty basin up, fighting not to cringe as it slammed into her kneecap on the way.

Calm down, woman, she thought.

Dear god, this man made her bones hum.

She marched back toward the saloon door, the laughter and hollering now a muffled chorus in the distance beyond the sound of her blood pulsing in her ears. She passed within a foot of Shannon on her way to the door, fighting to keep her eyes straight. His hand was at her elbow then, and the sensation felt so charged, she lost her grip on the basin handle again, and it crashed to the dirt with a clang. He tugged her hard enough to throw her off balance but caught her as she slammed into his chest.

"Do you want me to kiss you, Cady?"

She swallowed, fighting to find words of agreement or protest – anything. He gazed down at her, his whispers gravelly and searing like hot coals.

She finally found the will to speak, and the most senseless words fell from her lips. “My name’s Cadence. Not Cady.”

He chuckled, his canines catching on his lower lip as he smiled. “I do apologize.”

“Sorry, that was rude. Sorry. It’s just – my Mama gave me that name on purpose. Everyone’s always tryin to turn it into a girl’s name. But that ain’t my name, you know -?”

Shannon leaned down and pressed his lips to hers, stilling her nervous rambling. He was right, he tasted like pipe tobacco – a sweet, spicy sort. Cadence leaned into him, her legs hardly holding her weight beneath her. Shannon curled his fingers into her hair and doubled his effort, pulling her against him in such a way that Cadence felt her heart stop. No man had ever wrapped around her like that before – with the fury of wanting her. She felt warm and emboldened by it. She clutched the back of his coat, letting the smell of pipe tobacco and bourbon – and something like honey - surround her.

She squealed softly as his tongue pierced her mouth, flitting against her own. She tensed against him, so startled by the sensation, and by how good it felt. He held her tightly, as though he feared she would pull away at that moment, and continued his exploration of her mouth, his tongue seeking hers. She let her body rest against him, like some pillar of stone.

Finally, he took her face in his hands and pulled from her lips to look down at her. This man that towered over her, with his graceful way and his foreboding presence. He seemed so gentle in that moment, gazing down at her as though pleasantly surprised.

The corner of Shannon's mouth turned up on one side with a sly grin. "I'll never misspeak your name again."

She sighed. Just as he leaned into her to kiss her again, another bout of laughter splintered the silent city air. They both straightened, turning in the direction of the sound.

Cadence pulled from his arms, remembering herself. "Cal will be getting ornery inside. I've got chores that need doin."

Shannon leaned back against the wall. "Will I see you again?"

"If ya like? I mean, ya certainly know where to find me."

He shook his head. "I mean tonight."

"What?" She said, blurting it out with such shrill force that a drunk in the distance hooted back at her.

"I'd like to kiss you more," he said.

"Ya would?" Her knees all but gave out beneath her, but she stayed upright. She pressed her thighs together, feeling a sudden tingling sensation travel down her belly to between her legs. "Well, I mean -"

"I do not mean to be so forthright, but – I find you captivating, Cadence."

Cadence stared at him.

What kind of man tells a woman she's captivating? Is he a snake oil salesmen? That's just too good a line, she thought.

"I ain't nothing special."

Shannon took her hand and kissed her knuckles. Then he shot her a devilish look, his lips still pressed to her hand. "You go on and finish your chores. If you'd like to spend more time with me this evenin, I'll be right here."

Cadence swallowed, listening for sounds within the saloon. There was no hollering. Calvin seemed ensconced in the profit from such a busy night, and he had Maxwell and Persephone to help out.

And damn it, it's my name on the damn deed. It's my saloon! I can do as I damn well, please.

Cadence kicked the basin aside and threw herself against Shannon's chest, wrapping her arms around his neck. He slumped back into the wall of the saloon, grinning wide as she kissed him, her lips grazing his teeth. He quickly wrapped his arms around her, half lifting her off the ground as he pulled her against him. Cadence opened her mouth, waiting. "Do that thing with your tongue, again."

His body shook against her as he chuckled. "Oh, if you like that, you'll love all the other things I can do with my tongue."

That same tingling sensation returned, but now it was tripled in force. Cadence wasn't completely innocent. She'd known that sensation before, once in the back room of the post office with Stephen Goldrup, the young man who sorted the mail. They'd knocked over a sack of mail, and she ended up with splinters in her backside from the store room floor. Then later, they'd run off into the woods a few times to fumble with each other again. It hurt the first two times, lasted only a couple minutes, and seemed more than a little overrated to hear Persephone or Dolores speak of it, but she felt the tingle between her legs each time when Stephen gave her that knowing look. They might've continued with their tryst, but Stephen Goldrup left to work on a ranch some forty miles out of town and married the rancher's thirty-year-old daughter. That was years ago, and Cadence hadn't been touched since.

She hadn't thought to miss it much – until now.

What kind of woman would Shannon think she was if he knew she wanted more than a kiss?

He kissed her and teased her with his tongue, darting into her mouth as she squirmed and squealed in protest. She could feel his laughter in his chest, feel his teeth bared over and over as he smiled into the kiss. Strange how this stranger had gone from as foreboding as gun smoke in the air, to as assuring as a purring cat in her lap. A purring cat that she was sure could turn and bite at any time. Still, she didn't feel afraid.

Shannon pulled from her eager lips after moments of kissing. Her chin and lips were raw from the rough texture of his stubble, and she was sure her skin was flushed red from it.

She cared little. She didn't want to stop.

Shannon glanced down the alleyway in both directions, dodging her lips as she tried to kiss him again. His face cracked in one of the warmest smiles she'd ever seen.

"Would you have me take you here in the dark, Duchess?"

Cadence stopped, taking in the alleyway anew. There were puddles of sludge from the mud of the road, the waste water of the saloon, and any number of passing drunkards who thought to stop and take a piss on their way through. The smell of the place betrayed all of that, but she'd been too lost in the way Shannon tasted to care.

"Oh, uh – no. S'pose I wouldn't."

He gently let go of her, brushing a strand of hair from her face. "I didn't think so."

She grabbed his hand from her cheek and held it, playing with his fingers nervously. She didn't know how to say what she wanted. This man wasn't a Stephen Goldrup. Shannon was a full grown, experienced man. He kissed like it, too. She wanted to feel the burn of his stubble on her chin some more.

"I got a room – upstairs?"

Her nerves stifled the words in her throat, making them half the volume she'd intended. Still, it seemed Shannon heard her loud and clear because he grabbed her hand and yanked her toward the back door of the saloon, a mischievous grin on his face.

She fought to stifle her giggles as they careened down the hall and up the back stairs. Cadence listened as they rushed away from the saloon, sure she'd hear Calvin's voice calling after her, demanding she come back and finish some chore or another. Yet, there was no sound save for their shoes on the wooden steps. Shannon stopped at the top of the stairs, pulling her toward him again to kiss her. He planted his hands squarely on her backside and squeezed, kissing her through her startled shriek. He loosened his hold on her and grinned, his eyes twinkling in the half-light.

His energy had changed. He no longer carried that wary intensity or that warning glare. He'd descended into an almost youth-like excitement as he glanced down the hall in both directions, waiting for her to point the way. She was enjoying him, immensely.

"Last door on the lef -"

He grabbed her and dragged her down the hall, slamming her back into the door of her bedroom. He had an almost constant smile on his face now, and he reached down her back to grab her ass again.

Stephen Goldrup had never touched her like this.

He turned the knob at her hip and caught her as she leaned backward into the open doorway. Her room was dim, barely lit by moonlight through the window panes. Shannon kicked her bedroom door shut behind them and pulled his coat open, shrugging it down his shoulders with impatience.

Cadence's stomach instantly tightened. She wanted him – desperately. Still, the air between them felt so thick and loaded with possibility now, she almost couldn't breathe. Shannon moved to pull his shirt from the waist of his trousers, but Cadence couldn't move. She felt frozen suddenly, watching as his body language betrayed every intention. Shannon moved toward her now and she stepped back, inhaling sharply.

"What is it? Is something wrong?" He asked, still betraying a half smile.

Cadence stared at him, unable to make out his eyes beyond a tiny pinprick of white reflected in his irises. She splayed her hands out before her, wanting to touch him, but too nervous to attempt.

He chuckled there in the dark. "Am I meant to stop?"

"No," she said, blurting it out with more desperation than she'd intended.

"Would you have me take you in hand, then?"

Why did those words unsettle her so? The answer was yes, but she wanted to scream it. Good lord, how desperately she wanted to be taken in hand, and unlike fumbling Stephen Goldrup, she was sure Shannon could do it.

She felt her hands begin to tremble. How would it feel? If Persephone was to be believed – it would be life changing.

"Is my door locked?" She asked.

Shannon went to the door, and she heard the faint click as the bolt slid into place. Her heart raced with such fury, she could feel it in her ears.

"Are you a maiden, Cadence?"

"What? No!" She stopped, cringing at the shrillness of her response. "I mean, I ain't been all over town or nothin, but – this ain't my first time if that's what you're insinuatin."

Shannon smiled, and the white bar of his teeth lit up the room even in the dark. "I insinuate nothing, petal. Then if you tell me 'Yes,' I'll ravish you on every surface in the room."

Cadence's knees buckled beneath her, and she toppled into her reading chair.

Shannon gave a soft laugh, coming across the room toward her with a calm gait. He dropped down to his knees, the floorboards creaking beneath him. She felt his hands envelop her ankles, and she stiffened. Then his hands moved up the length of her calves until his fingers grazed the back of her knees, drawing a panicked ticklish response there. She jerked in the chair, trying to take hold of his hands beneath her skirts.

"You remember that thing I do with my tongue?" He said.

Cadence whimpered softly as her confidence evaporated. She could barely nod her response.

"Well," he said, and his hands ran up the outside of her thighs beneath her skirts. He took hold of the waistband of her petticoats. "I consider myself a man of my word."

He flashed her a wicked grin and tugged her undergarments down the length of her thighs before she even realized he'd moved. Cadence scrambled to push her skirts between her legs, but Shannon quickly tossed her skirts up over her lap and planted his palms against the inside of her thighs, pushing them apart. She felt so exposed suddenly, so vulnerable. What on earth did this man intend to do to her on his knees?

Shannon reached up her skirts further, grabbing her hips, and yanked her toward him, nearly pulling her straight off the chair. She squealed again, but the sound was stilled instantly as Shannon lunged toward her, his face disappearing beneath her skirts.

She felt the stubble of his cheeks graze against her thigh just an instant before the warmth of his tongue pressed against her, parting her to him. She screamed, gripping the arms of the chair to pull away.

What kind of man does something like this?

She tried to close her legs around him, but he just pressed his face against her harder as his left hand reached up and clamped over her mouth. She continued to shriek into the calloused skin of his hand, but her cries were losing their tenacity, sinking to a much more shocked and delighted place. He moved against her with such purpose, she almost feared he might bite her, groaning and chuckling softly to himself from beneath her skirts. She fought with the nervous thoughts – of what she must taste like – and her breathing grew sharper as she fought to catch her breath.

She caught a subtle metallic tinge - the scent from his hand.

Suddenly, his smiling eyes appeared from beneath her skirts, and he loosened his hold over her mouth. "Are you finished screaming?"

She swallowed, finding it hard to meet his gaze knowing what an intimate thing he now knew of her – of how she tasted. Cadence took a shaky breath and nodded. Shannon saw the gesture, snatched up her skirts, and lifted them up onto her, leaving her bared to the dark room. Then he planted his mouth on her again, his breath coming in sharp bursts as he laughed, shooting her that same wicked look when he slid his fingers inside her. She clamped her own hand over her mouth to still her cries.

He felt like nothing she'd ever had with Stephen Goldrup. Dear god, what sort of man would touch a woman the way Shannon was touching her? Not even Persephone or Dolores warned of this sort of thing.

Cadence fought to still her whimpers and hold still, but she found her hips moving against him. He shot her another look, his mouth still hard at work as he glared up at her. The look rattled her to her center. Had she known a man could look at her like that – make her feel the way Shannon made her feel, she'd have never given Stephen Goldrup a second go.

Cadence leaned back in the chair, letting her legs fall apart to him. He doubled his efforts, the groans of his own pleasure making it impossible not to shake beneath him. She didn't understand Shannon's pleasure in doing this, but with the warmth of his touch spreading across her belly, inspiring her insides to tighten with such sudden intensity, she didn't care. She just wanted him to keep going.

Cadence's head fell back, and she opened her mouth in a silent scream, her legs twitching at his shoulders. She inhaled deeply, the metal scent now heavier with each passing moment.

She startled, feeling Shannon pull from her as her convulsions slowed. The metallic smell unnerved her suddenly, and she quickly gathered her skirts, straining to focus in the dark.

Were Shannon's hands dark? She couldn't tell.

The moment of release and pleasure had given way to panic and embarrassment.

The metal in the air smelled familiar. It smelled like blood.

Cadence silently began to pray that Shannon wouldn't be mortified to find her bleeding all over him. The passionate abandon she'd felt a moment ago had died, instantly.

Shannon wiped a hand over his stubbled face and leaned into her, coming close enough to kiss her again. She let him, and for the moment he was close to her lips, the smell of blood disappeared, leaving just the scent of his breath, bourbon, and her.

He stopped suddenly, and she was sure he'd noticed her sudden change in demeanor. Shannon straightened up, his hands resting gently on her thighs. He glanced back to the closed door as though half expecting someone to enter. Cadence watched him in silence.

"Can you give me a minute, beautiful?" He asked.

Cadence sat up, her unease shifting to something far more worrisome than just having her monthly. "Of course."

Shannon leaned into her again, planting a deep, lingering kiss on her lips before he pinched her chin and turned for the door. Cadence sat still until he was out of the room and the door closed behind him. She snatched up her skirts and slid her fingers between her legs. Then she turned, holding her wet fingers to the light of the window. They glistened, but there was no trace of blood. She sighed in such relief, she almost melted out of the chair.

Cadence waited for another moment, then decided to move to the bed. When he returned, she wanted to waste no time in having the rest of him.

Another long moment passed, and Cadence began to worry. If Shannon went to freshen up, or relieve himself, he was taking a good long time, and Cadence hadn't heard the familiar sounds of Calvin heading up to bed. If Calvin headed up now, and the two men crossed paths, she'd be in a world of trouble.

Cadence lay there listening to the sounds of the world.

There was only silence.

She rose from her bed, worried. Was Calvin silently holding Shannon at gunpoint in the hallway? Or worse, had Shannon up and left her, deciding she tasted like getting the hell outta dodge.

She turned the doorknob slowly, as though making noise might offend this weighted quiet. The door opened and the metallic smell flooded through the open door, overwhelming her. Cadence's stomach turned, instantly.

"Shannon," she called, softly. She wanted him. At that moment, she wanted the heaviness of his presence to surround her – protect her from the uneasiness she felt.

There was no response.

Cadence stepped out into the hallway in her bare feet, feeling her way along the wall in the near dark. "Shannon," she called again. Still, there was no response.

She made her way down the steps to the back hallway of the saloon and felt her spine tense. The smell was getting stronger now.

It's not blood, she thought. It can't be. One would have to slaughter a whole pig to cause such a strong smell in the air. Yet there was no other source her mind could conjure – a warm copper smell tinged with something more, something living.

Cadence stepped out into the open room of the saloon and felt something ooze between her bare toes before she could take in what lay before her.

Shannon was there, crouched down by the bar, his hands almost black with blood, and beneath him lay the familiar form of Calvin Hoover, an open cavity where his chest had once been.

Cadence inhaled sharply, and Shannon lunged from where he perched, his bloodied hand splayed before him as he reached out toward her.

"You will not scream!" He hissed.

Cadence opened her mouth wide, her whole body humming with terror at what she saw, but no sound came. She inhaled, desperation building in her chest, but again no sound came. She couldn't scream. She wanted to, needed to, but with each deeper inhale, her lungs refused the work.

Shannon returned to the form lying prone by the bar. Cadence couldn't move, her feet still pressed firmly into the pool of blood beneath her. She found the will to look down at her red stained feet and saw a trail of blood leading away from her. She followed it with her eyes, her throat growing tighter with each inch of distance she covered. She knew what she would find at the end of the trail. She wasn't ready.

Persephone lay sprawled across the floor by the stage, her dress ripped open, her breasts bared, a gaping hole of blood and viscera just beneath her ribs. Just beside Persephone's ravaged body, blood was dripping down the wall from the stage. Cadence couldn't see what lay on the stage just out of sight, but she didn't dare move. However awful – however desperate she was to deny her instincts, to deny the very thing that was happening around her, Cadence was sure what lay just out of sight was her friend Maxwell's corpse, equally torn asunder.

She watched Shannon's hands move, something glinting in his right hand as he pulled something from Calvin's chest. Cadence turned away, feeling her throat tighten. She was bent over against the wall a moment later, her dinner splattered across the sideboard.

"Cadence."

She couldn't move. Shannon was calling to her, his voice strained, but she couldn't look at him. How could she have let such a monster touch her? How could she have been so fooled?

A burst of sound startled them both toward the saloon doors. Now locked, there were passersby coming close to the doors, their drunken laughter echoing down the street. The saloon was darkened now, but the carnage would be visible if someone came to the window to look closely. Cadence stepped toward the doors, her mouth opening to call for help, but again she was mute. She was compelled by his words. Somehow, she couldn't disobey.

"Cadence, look at me."

She spun away, pressing her back to the wall and shutting her eyes tight as Shannon came toward her. She could feel him near, his presence still felt immense, still overwhelming, but now it had taken on a dark weight. This man had torn everyone she cared about to pieces. What would he do to her?

"Open your eyes," Shannon said, his voice barely a whisper as the voices outside began to grow in volume. They were coming closer.

Cadence did as she was told, helpless to deny him his request. It was as though his words became law as soon as he spoke them. The sense of helplessness was almost more terrifying than the thought of being his next victim. She met his gaze, his dark eyes wet and his brow furrowed. He looked as panicked as she felt.

She turned her head away, but he took hold of her jaw in his bloodied fingers, turning her to face him.

"Look at me. Listen to me. Cadence, I'm not going to hurt you."

She shook again, trying to deny the sight of him.

"Listen to me. I am sorry. Please, believe me. I would never wish to compel you, but -" The sounds outside crescendoed and Cadence jerked away from him.

Shannon held her face in his hands, the blood congealing and growing sticky on her skin.

Tears were streaming down her cheeks as he drew closer.

"Please look at me, Cadence."

She'd always loved the way her name sounded when he said it. Now, it was unnerving to hear.

Still, she did as she was asked, but unlike before, this felt like a choice. Shannon's eyes betrayed something pained, as though he was helpless to his own madness.

Shannon moved closer, whispering as the voices rose outside. "I would never hurt you. I'm sorry for what I'm about to do."

Cadence's eyes darted around the room, terrified, willing herself far away as she braced for her death.

He rushed back over to Calvin who lay face up on the floor, then Shannon shot her a look, his brow furrowed. "Look away, petal."

Her head turned without choice, but even from the corner of her eye, she caught sight of Shannon grabbing up the piano bench. She listened to his footsteps, then cringed, a cry escaping softly as a sickening sound filled the room – like the sound of a melon being split. The sound came several more times, each time layered with a wet, sticky softness that absorbed the brunt of the hit. Though she could not see, and could not force herself to look, she knew Shannon was pummeling Calvin with the piano bench.

Why? Why would he do something so foul – the man was dead already? For the love of God! Leave him be, she thought.

"Open your mouth, Cadence."

She startled to find him so close again, feeling the compulsion of his words work through her. She cried softly as she opened her mouth.

"Trust me, do this for me, and I promise I will never – no one will ever be able to compel you again."

She helplessly did as she was told, whimpering as Shannon's hand moved toward her face. He slipped something onto her tongue – a warm, wet, and almost slithery something. Cadence felt her throat tighten again in wait of being sick.

"Swallow, Cadence."

Her eyes went wide as her body obeyed his word over her own disgust. She was helpless to deny him – enslaved by an utterance.

What kind of foul magic was this?

She felt the rubbery piece of flesh slide down her throat, and she yelped softly in disgust as it settled into her belly.

Shannon turned her face to him again, looking down at her with intent. "Wait 'til I'm gone, Duchess. Please. Then scream your pretty little head off."

Then he was gone, moving so swiftly she almost didn't see him disappear out the back door of the saloon and out into the alley. From there he could slip unseen to anywhere – the main streets, or off to the woods or ranches in the outskirts of town. He'd be gone before anyone would think to look, and there she stood in the silent saloon surrounded by the gore of dark deeds.

And she wasn't screaming.

He'd told her to scream, but unlike before, she wasn't compelled by his word. When she screamed now, it would be a choice.

She heaved over, sticking her finger down her throat, ready to purge whatever dark communion he'd made her take. Yet she stopped, her finger perched just at the tip of her tongue. She bent over again, readied for the violence of being sick, but the action itself, the desperate need to purge this piece of her stepfather – it died each time she readied for the deed. She couldn't make herself be sick. Her eyes welled up with tears as she barely glanced over her shoulder at the crimes around her and opened her mouth.

There with the blood of her stepfather drying on her skin, Cadence loosed the most desperate wail her lungs had ever mustered.

CHAPTER THREE

"CHRIST, WHAT DID THEY do to him?" A male voice cried out in the saloon, followed by the pathetic sounds of retching. Cadence heard that sound more that morning than on all other days of her life combined. The scene within the saloon was a powerful one.

"I told you, his name was Shannon," she mumbled, hardly able to form the words.

Just saying his name gave her the shivers. Cadence sat in the back room of her saloon, listening to the footsteps and hushed voices of deputies moving out in the main parlor. The sound of someone getting sick echoed through the room again, followed by another man's voice scolding the poor fellow who'd lost his constitution.

Sheriff Sharples paced back and forth from the open saloon door, glancing out at the carnage with each pass as though he expected it to set itself to sorts. "Yes, you said that. Any idea where he would have gone?"

She shook her head. "I didn't know him too well."

"No? Then what was he doing here so late?"

She managed to shoot the Sheriff a glare. Seth Sharples wasn't born in Wyoming, but had come by way of Pennsylvania, and everything about him screamed pompous Easterner – at least it did to her. Calvin had fought for the Confederates during the Civil War, and he called anyone from the North a Yankee the entire time she'd known him.

Or he had.

Cadence frowned.

"He a friend of your Pa's?"

Cadence shook her head. "I'd say that's an obvious no, ain't it?"

Despite her wish for ignorance, when the drunk men barged into the saloon that night, hell-bent on finding and fixing the source of her screams, they'd each, in turn, recoiled at the sight of Calvin's body. Their reaction forced her to look, knowing what she would find. Shannon had bashed Calvin's face in with the piano bench. The only thing to identify him was the bar towel hanging at his belt.

"He a friend of yours, then?"

Cadence didn't get a chance to snap back as another man slipped into the room, a handkerchief over his mouth as he passed one of the younger deputies. The smell in the saloon was beginning to change – the sour smell of old blood and worse. Apparently, bodies didn't stop certain processes when they died, and the stench of shit was mingling now with the metallic curdle of open wounds.

"Can I help you, Detective?" Sharples asked the new man. The detective shot her an appraising look before flicking his handkerchief out and tucking it back into his pocket.

"No, but I thought I might be of some assistance to you."

The two men turned to one another and began to confer without her. She could hear their voices, but felt distant, as though listening to passersby in a dream. She looked down at her hands; they were shaking.

"Not sure how they do things in Chicago, but here we have a way -"

"It's just a suggestion. With the Packer fellow in custody – given his proclivities..."

Both men went silent, and Cadence gave them a closer look.

Sharples glanced her way, frowning.

"We might have a downright panic on our hands if word gets out there's more than one cannibal in town."

Cadence swallowed hard, remembering the intruder that now festered in her stomach.

She cringed, wishing she could've made herself sick. Damn it, Cadence. You should've tried harder, she thought.

Sharples glared at the detective. "Who said anything about cannibals -?"

A young deputy, redheaded with a flush to his face just as red, turned out the door of the backroom and into the carnage to get away from the Sheriff.

"I'm just saying. Three corpses with their hearts cut out? Pieces of them missing? Are you telling me that wouldn't cause a panic?"

The Sheriff sighed. "Well, what would you suggest, Finkbone? You're here to investigate cattle thieving, not -"

"Tell me you have the manpower to handle this without me and I'm gone," the man named Finkbone said.

Cadence stared at their feet, lost in a sea of fog. A moment of weighted silence passed in the crowded space, then they seemed to come to an accord.

The new man's face appeared before her, leaning to take a knee. "Cadence, is it? I'm Detective John Finkbone. You can call me John, of course. Oh goodness. Seth, do you have a handkerchief to let this poor thing get cleaned up?"

Cadence swallowed, hardly giving him a glance, but a wet rag was offered a moment later. She could hardly feel the blood now. It had dried and nearly hardened along the length of her jaw. She reached up to her face, touching the wet fabric to her skin idly. One pass and the effort was too much to continue. Det. Finkbone took the rag from her hand and began to gently wipe her face.

"I'm sorry you've gone through this, poor girl, but can you tell us anything further about the gentleman who did this?"

Cadence stared at her hands, an image of Shannon rushing to mind. Despite what she'd seen - when she let him come to mind, she saw that mischievous grin, the way his eyes glinted when he looked up at her from between her legs. She cringed.

Finkbone frowned. "Sorry, girl. I know this must be difficult for you."

"You called for me?"

Cadence glanced up to the new voice in the room and found Cecil Tennet standing in the doorway as pale as a sheet. His partner, the lawyer Malcolm Green, stood beside him, his face a color befitting his name.

"What the hell are they doin here?" Cadence asked, her hackles instantly up. She knew Cecil as a customer, but his leisure time was only a fraction of his reasons for coming to the Red Onion. The bank of Cheyenne had moved into Main Street, and ever since then, Tennet & Green had their eyes on the Red Onion. They'd offered Calvin a pretty penny more than once to take over the property, but given it wasn't Calvin's name on the deed, Cadence had threatened murderous response to Calvin for even humoring the uptight pricks of T&G.

"Nothing for you to worry your pretty head over, dear. Now, what can you tell me about this man? What was his name, you said – Shannon? Any notion of his last name?"

"Bell!" The word came from a memory she didn't even realize she had. "And I said what the hell are y'all doin here?"

Tennet was eyeing the room with interest as Green simply fought to keep his lunch down. Cadence knew damn well these pricks had no reason to be at such a scene save for one.

"You've no right! You hear me?" She screamed.

Cadence was on her feet now, her mind racing. Where was the deed? Where was her Mama's will? They had no right to the place, and she wasn't planning to sell, but no one knew the saloon was in her name. The only man who did lay dead on the floor less than five yards from where she stood.

"Young lady, you need to calm down," Sharples said sternly, but Cadence was across the room, lunging for Green. He was clearly the less solid man at that moment, and she was still covered in blood.

"I want you out - both of you! You got no business bein here!"

Cecil's white face twitched. "Madam, this establishment is now property of the state -"

Cecil hadn't the chance to finish his sentence before Cadence went for him. She clawed at his face, feeling the skin tear beneath her fingers before arms enveloped her waist, yanking her back.

"I'll kill you, you fucker! I swear to God, you come near what's mine, and I'll rip your god damn throat out, you son of a bitch!"

"Ms. Hoover!" Detective Finkbone said, shock easily read in his voice. Cadence fought against his hold, lunging toward the banker and his lawyer as Malcolm Green lost his fight with sickness and dashed from the room. Cecil stood just out of her reach as Finkbone lifted Cadence up to hold her back.

"Damn it, Finkbone. She's hysterical! Get her out of here! Girl needs the infirmary!"

"I'll fucking kill you!" Cadence screamed one more time as Finkbone heaved her over his shoulder and carried her out into the saloon. The fury in her heart drowned out the horror's around her as the detective carried her through the blood-soaked room.

She kicked violently, screaming in protest. She couldn't leave. She had to go upstairs. She had to get the deed to show them. They had to see reason.

Yet John Finkbone was stronger, and he hauled out into the main street of Cheyenne, her hysteria drawing curious stares from passersby as Finkbone stuffed her into a carriage.

Cadence fought with her 'captors,' calling them scoundrels and bitches with each attempt to calm or feed her. The doctor had ordered she remain in the infirmary for a span of two days, his expert opinion being that she would calm with time and healthy meals – and medication. Cadence could barely eat anything they put in front of her. She fought with the nurses until the doctor made her drink laudanum. Once the laudanum set in, she was too dreamy to argue with much of anything.

As a result of their constant supervision, Cadence slept for much of the two days she spent in the infirmary.

The detective came again, asking the same questions she'd answered multiple times.

"Yes, I'm sure he said his name was Shannon Bell," she'd assured him.

A deputy came through to offer a few items from home, but she was too out of sorts to take note.

Her heart hurt in such furious ways. She ached to think of the suffering that befell her friends, ached to know she'd never see Maxwell's sad attempts at a magic show, or Persephone winking over the shoulder of some bearded mark. She even ached to think her ornery stepfather wouldn't be behind the bar when she returned home, but above all of those things, she ached to know she'd let such a monster slither his way into her heart.

She'd wanted him beyond just a man's touch. Cadence had found Shannon irresistible from the moment he set foot into that saloon. How could she have been so wrong about a man?

How could she ever trust another knowing how faulty her heart's compass could be?

She was heartbroken, and she'd only known the beast for a week.

By the third day, she'd learned to placate her nurses with a seeming calm, but she was determined to find her focus. She let her insides turn to fire, distracting herself with the desperate need to get back to her saloon. She needed to find her Mama's will and the deed, and she needed to prepare for war.

And she needed to drown out the memory of the gunpowder voiced man.

"Do you have anyone to walk you home, dear?"

"Everyone I know is dead," Cadence said, the deadpan of her voice clearly unnerving the nurse behind the desk.

"Well, um," the nurse said, swallowing between words. "You're sure you're feeling well enough- ?"

"Can I have my effects?" Cadence interrupted, holding her hands out. The nurse placed a brown paper wrapped bundle into Cadence's arms – her petticoats, a pair of socks, and pins that were in her hair when she arrived.

Cadence pulled the package to her chest and turned on her heel, heading out the door of the dismal infirmary. She turned onto Main Street a block away and started marching toward home.

The roads bustled as they always did, men heading to and from ranches, mines, and banks, making a point to shoot her a sideways glance as she passed. Women rarely walked through town unaccompanied, and were it a darker hour, she might've been concerned for her welfare, but their looks were no more concerned than that.

Was it true? Had the Sheriff really hidden what happened in the Red Onion saloon from his county?

"Pardon me, miss?"

Cadence stiffened, straightening her back as she kept walking. She wouldn't be approached by some leering prick today of all days.

"Miss Cadence? Might I have a word?"

She shot half a glance over her shoulder and nearly stumbled on a wobbly board in the sidewalk. The familiar native man lunged forward, his arms out in wait to catch her. She steadied herself, taking several steps away from him.

His expression had softened since last she saw him, but his black hair was just as long as she remembered it. He now held the wide brimmed hat in his hands, letting her see the smooth contours of his brown face. She'd half-forgotten her savior from the alley.

She pressed her back to the railing of the sidewalk before turning toward home again. "I doubt I'd have anything of interest to talk about."

The native man caught up to her, matching her stride. "Well, I promise not to take much of your time. I have questions -"

"You and everybody else. Look, I don't know nothin! And what the hell interest would *you* have in my affairs?"

"I believe we've both been crossed by the same man."

Cadence stopped, the sun beating down on her brow from the east. She turned to face him and found his dark eyes unnervingly sincere. "What man would that be?"

"The one known as Shannon Bell."

Cadence nearly dropped the bundle, but she steadied herself. Just the sound of his name still shook her to her core. "What of him?"

"I am – we were associates."

The man's voice had a different rhythm than the white men she knew, but his English was perfect. "Well, congrats. I don't suppose I have to tell you just what kind of man he was?" She said, picking up her step again.

"No, I don't believe you do. There are stories around the city that something – dark took place at your establishment."

"Is that so? Just stories? Man tore everyone I love to pieces is what happened."

"I am sorry, miss. I know you lost your father. I did not mean -"

"Oh, it's fine. I weren't talkin about him." Cadence stopped, startled by the cavalier sound of her own words. This determination to distract herself from her grief was clearly working better than she'd intended.

"Oh," the man said, catching her stride as she took off again.

Cadence swallowed, almost ashamed at her callous tone. "It weren't that I didn't – I mean. He weren't my Pa."

She struggled with her addled thoughts at that moment. She'd cared for Calvin, but he'd never sought her love, and she'd never offered it. Theirs was a business relationship and little more than that.

Persephone and Maxwell, on the other hand, had been her only close friends. Hell, if Maxwell hadn't preferred the company of men, he might've been much more than just a friend.

Cadence shook her head, trying to loose the thoughts.

None of that mattered now. She had to set her affairs in order. Until that was done, there was no time to mourn.

"Is there somewhere I might ask you some questions – in private?"

She turned on the man, frowning. "Fine. You can come in the saloon. Might be more than a little unpleasant. I ain't sure how much cleanin's been done."

The native man followed her around the corner into view of the Red Onion. Just the sight of the front deck gave her pause.

Was she ready to set foot in that place again?

An instant later, she noticed the wide open front doors of the saloon, and all apprehension was gone, giving way to panic and fury. She stormed up the front steps and into the parlor.

The wood floors, stage wall, and bar were scrubbed to such a sheen, they looked brand new, and behind the bar, a workman stood taking demands from a familiar smug bastard.

"Cecil, God damn it!" She bellowed.

Cadence moved across the saloon floor, her fists clenched tight at her sides. She barely took her third step before hands had a hold of her elbows, pulling her back from the bar.

Cecil barely glanced over, conferring with the workmen who hovered in the backroom. "Take it up with the state, Miss Hoover. The law's the law."

She ripped her hands free of her captors and crossed the bar. "The law my ass! My name's on the deed, you soft prick!"

"I highly suggest you calm down," Cecil said, his calm tone grating on every nerve.

She shook against the hands that took hold of her arms again, trying to free herself from the thugs' hold. "Calm down? I'm going to end you!"

The two ruffians tugged her backward, leading her back out the door. She struggled against them, aching to get up those damn stairs and into her bedroom, but there was no fighting them. If they didn't want her there, she had no choice but to comply.

"You son of a bitch, Cecil! You've no right! I'll have you take your hands off me and get outta my place! The Red Onion is fucking mine!"

She was out in the sunshine a moment later, standing there with two massive thugs between her and the saloon doors. She imagined biting them, fighting them, climbing them like trees and tearing their ears off like picking apples, but they were huge, and though she wasn't as young as she looked, she was not a giant among men.

Cadence glared up at them, then watched helplessly as they turned and went back into the saloon. She felt her chest growing tight, and her face contorted.

No, you bitch. You are not gonna cry in the street! You hear me? Don't you dare cry!

Cadence turned back up the road. It was only then that she realized the native man was gone.

They couldn't keep her out of her own home. There were laws. She had a deed! She thought.

She turned the corner again and headed up the way toward the office of Malcolm Green. He was Cecil's partner, and he knew the law better than anyone. When he heard the deed was in her name, he'd tell his rat faced partner to back off, wouldn't he?

He had to.

Malcolm Green's office was upstairs from a small barber shop, a temporary location while he and Tennet put their affairs in order. Even in the temporary space, Malcolm Green was holding court.

"Yes, I'm well aware of your situation, Miss Hoover."

"My name ain't Hoover."

Malcolm's eyebrows shot up. "Is that so?"

"Calvin weren't my Pa. My Pa's name was Delacouer."

Malcolm rifled through a few papers by the window, then sauntered back to his seat behind the desk. Cadence kept her perch dutifully, despite the anxious energy that surged through every inch of her.

Malcolm settled on a pair of folded and yellowed papers. "Ah yes. Here we are."

He sat down across from her and set the papers down. He stared down at them for a long moment, silent.

"Well?"

Mr. Green shot her a half grin look, then seemed to catch himself, straightening his lips to a tightly pursed look of disinterest. "Well, you see – Mrs. Hoover did clearly state you were to receive the saloon upon event of her death -"

"I told you!"

"But you know as well as I do a woman can't write a will."

Cadence straightened. "What the hell does that mean?"

"The will, wherever it might be, is a lovely piece of legal prose, my dear, but a woman has no legal right to will property. Without a male heir to inherit, any property that may have been hers would revert to the state."

"But my name's on the deed!"

Malcolm raised an eyebrow. "And do you have this piece of paper on your person?"

Cadence swallowed, almost choking to get the words out. "No, but I'll have it as soon as I can get back into the Onion -"

Malcolm snorted softly. "Miss Hoover."

"Delacouer!" She hollered.

Malcolm gave her a tolerant smile. "Without the deed, and without Calvin here to either back your claim or transfer ownership to you, I'm afraid there's nothing I can do. My hands are tied."

"I'm tellin you, it's mine! The Red Onion is mine! Mama put it in my name before she died! Why won't you believe me?"

Malcolm shook his head, the same laughter of the mildly entertained. "It's not a matter of believing you. The law is the law. You don't have the deed, so legally, once she married your fath - stepfather, the saloon would have become his rightful property. Therefore, any transfer of ownership would need to be done by him now. Without the deed, those are the facts, sadly."

Cadence's throat tightened again. She'd be damned if she'd let this man see her cry. "My Pa had it in his will, didn't he? It's in there somewhere! They both made damn sure it would be mine. Mine and no one else's!"

Mr. Green rose from his desk and crossed the small office. He opened the glass door to his receiving area, holding it open to her as he waited for her to take the hint and leave. "I am truly sorry Miss Delacouer, but ownership of the saloon has reverted to the state."

"Then why is Cecil fucking Tennet setting up residence in it?" She hollered, her voice cracking as she spoke.

"I'll ask you to refrain from such language in my office. I have neighbors with gentler sensibilities than a girl raised in a saloon."

"Tell me why he's there," she said, her words coming out in barely a whisper.

"The state will be auctioning off the property, and the auction is overseen entirely by the bank. I'm sorry, Cadence. Were your stepfather alive, he could transfer the ownership of the saloon to you, but he is not. And you have my condolences for that. Now if you don't mind, I need to prepare for my client."

He shot her a wide grin and waited. She sat as stone in that wooden chair, feeling it hum beneath her as her whole body shook. Cadence had never felt so furious – or so helpless. For an instant, she thought Malcolm Green made Shannon Bell look like a sleeping kitten.

How easily monsters hide in plain sight, she thought.

She stepped out into the front room and Malcolm Green closed the door behind her. She glanced around the room, feeling hopeless and lost. There was no one behind the small desk where Malcolm's assistant usually sat, and the walls were bare of any awards or degrees. She questioned just how Malcolm would benefit from the sale of the Red Onion – or worse, Cecil Tennet would do as he'd always planned and turn the place into another bank.

The greedy, cold-blooded scoundrels.

Cadence swayed there in silence, listening to Malcolm shuffle around inside his office. She searched the entire city in her mind for anyone who might wish her well – for anyone who might be on her side. There was no one. It was her against the world, and at that moment the head of that foul serpent was Cecil Tennet.

She had no other choice, and nothing left to lose. She would go plead her case to him, directly.

She had to try.

Cadence moved through the dirt streets by will alone. Somehow the argument with Malcolm had robbed the wind from her sails. She no longer felt righteously indignant. She felt wounded, betrayed – and alone. There was no one to comfort her or to seek out in hopes of a kind word or a hand up. She was alone, and every ounce of collateral she may have had was in a saloon she could no longer lay claim to, guarded by 'meat-headed pricks.'

If Malcolm Green was to be believed, just by being born a woman, she never had a claim to begin with. The world moved around her as it always did, but now, it felt as though each passing carriage or hat tipping cowhand moved in slow motion. The sheer size of her heart's burden felt back breaking. She was on her way to a conversation that would end any hope she had of a free life. If Cecil said the words, she was sure he would say, she was a single woman in the west.

Her choices were slim, to say the least.

She pulled her dress tight over her shoulders, only then realizing she'd left her bundle back at the saloon. Would Cecil even let her in the place to collect her things? If he knew there was a deed to be found, she feared not. Not even for clothes. Not even for a shawl and a change of petticoats.

The bank doors opened as she approached, men clearing out of the bank on their way home from making their weekly deposits. This was one of the days Calvin would make their own deposits.

Deposits in his own name or in the name of the saloon?

Was she at the very least entitled to his money?

The bank was busy with early business, and Cadence slipped past the counters to speak with Cecil's button-nosed assistant.

"Yes, he is in. If you'd take a seat, you can wait right here. He's with another customer."

Cadence's fire was all but lost now, and she slumped down into the chair with a heavy exhale. The bank went about its business around her, the bell over the wooden doors clanging with each newcomer. Cecil's assistant, Matilda, rose from her desk and disappeared into the back room, leaving Cadence to sit in the midst of this corner of the city, feeling haunted despite the cacophony of life around her.

Her brow furrowed and she turned her eyes to her fingers. She fidgeted with the fabric of her skirts. The man that sat beside her rustled his paper, shooting her a sideways glance over the corner of it. Her usual reaction to such wary glances was to glare right back. Cadence didn't care if it wasn't proper for a lady to be out in the city unaccompanied. She didn't care how that looked, or how loose her hair was, or how dainty and fragile she should be. Cadence had plenty reason to stand tall in the world of men – at least she thought she had.

Her status as 'Proprietor' was slipping from her fingers like water with each passing moment. Soon she'd have nothing. She wouldn't even have well-meaning friends to tell her to 'just marry a nice fella and have a few kids.'

She scolded herself softly as she contemplated her options.

She didn't scold herself for grieving. She scolded herself for Shannon.

She'd brought him into the Red Onion. She'd let him slip into the upstairs rooms with her while her friends went about their evening chores, innocent and oblivious to what was coming.

She remembered the tiny morsel of meat he'd made her consume and shuddered, clenching her fists. This naturally drew the eye of the man beside her again, but this time, he stood up, glared at her while he folded his paper, then dropped it onto his seat before walking away. All the lovely words she'd normally call after him came to mind, but she didn't speak a single one. Something far more important had stolen her attention.

The Colorado Cannibal

Alfred Packer, the notorious Cannibal of the Colorado Territory has been apprehended in Cheyenne. He was discovered living under the name John Schwartze -

Cadence skimmed these words because they were meaningless beside the words that had demanded her attention.

Packer will be transported to Colorado to face trial for the murders of Frank "Reddy" Miller, Israel Swann, James Humphreys, George Noon, and Shannon Wilson Bell.

Shannon Wilson Bell...

Cadence froze there, the words distorting on the page as she stared. She'd barely registered the words when the slow gait of the man leaving Cecil's office caught her attention. She didn't bother looking up, she was busy reading the accounts of Alfred Packer's crimes.

Cecil would call her in when he was ready – and when he had thugs to protect him, no doubt.

Packer alleges to having murdered Shannon Bell in self-defense after Bell slaughtered the rest of the party. Remains found in the Colorado Territory tell a different story.

Shannon Bell isn't dead!

The words were so powerful in her mind that she almost blurted them out for all to hear.

The man Packer claimed to have killed was no deader than she was.

She half wanted to march down to the paper and tell them so. No wonder he'd acted so strangely at Packer's arrest. Had he been afraid to be spotted because he was the true murderer? Or was Alfred lying and it was Shannon Bell who'd been the victim up there in the woods, surviving despite Packer's attempts to kill him as he had the others?

She shook her head against these thoughts as she tore the newspaper, carefully tearing this horrible section out to keep.

Cadence, you idiot. You've seen what Shannon is capable of. Packer's innocent. You have to tell someone!

The man leaving Cecil's office stopped just before her a moment. She didn't look up, focusing instead on tearing the piece of paper. Her head was swimming in too deep water for idle bank conversation.

His footsteps continued on, their gait so achingly slow that she wondered if he suffered some ailment.

The distance between them grew, and for an instant, she felt drawn in his direction, as though she could feel his eyes on her. Cadence furrowed her brow and looked up just in time to see Shannon Bell slip out the front doors of the bank.

Her voice caught in her throat. Should she scream for the deputies? Holler so the whole bank would know what walked among them?

Her heart shot into her throat with such fury, she feared she'd almost be sick. Cadence stood up from the bench, sending the paper flying across the floor as rage returned to her heart. She made a soft cry, but no words came. Her thoughts were racing too swiftly for words, and in amongst these racing thoughts, one idea barreled to the fore.

What business did Cecil Tennet have with the man that murdered her stepfather?

Had Cecil been behind the carnage at the Red Onion?

Cadence lunged around the assistant's empty desk and barged into Cecil's office, slamming the door behind her. "You son of a bitch, you better have a damn good explanation!"

She stopped dead as the familiar smell filled her nostrils.

The word came against her will. "No," she murmured, staring at Cecil's empty desk chair. "No, no. Please, no."

Cadence felt her hands shaking instantly as she moved around the corner of the desk. She caught sight of a well-made leather shoe sticking out from behind. She knew what she would find now. The horrors of the Red Onion replayed in her mind, sending her heart to pounding, yet she stepped forward.

Cecil Tennet lay there bleeding across the hardwood floor. Cadence dropped to her knees beside him, shaking him as though she might wake him from sleep. "Mr. Tennet? Oh god, Mr. Tennet?"

She pressed her hand to the blood soaked jacket and felt the fabric sink in. Cadence held her breath and lifted the jacket up from his blood-soaked chest. There was an open space – a black hole where the man's heart had been.

Shannon Bell had done his work again.

Cadence rose from the ground, her feet slipping in Cecil's blood as she began to cry out for help. The bank sounds stilled a moment in response, then changed as hurried footsteps came toward the office door. She pressed her hand against the glass, the doorknob slipping in her hand as she tried to flee the office, her fingers leaving trails of blood across the door. Panic was setting in. She was screaming now, unable to form words. She wanted to be away from this scene. She'd seen enough blood in the Red Onion for a lifetime. She'd never wanted to know that smell again. Yet here she was trapped with a corpse, his blood leaving her fingers too slick to open the damn door.

Her hand left a perfect bloodied print across the glass as the doorknob turned and someone freed her from outside.

"He's dead," she screamed as she fell out into the bank. "He's dead! He did it again!"

The men's voices changed to deeper, powerful concern as the few women present began to swoon and cry out. Someone let Cadence slump down, tearing their hands from her grasp. She felt the soaked fabric of her skirts against her ankles. She was covered in Cecil Tennet's blood.

"Get the Sheriff! Everyone step aside!" Someone yelled, and Cadence was lifted by strong arms and dragged across the length of the bank. Chaos ensued as men clamored to get closer to the office door, not out of a need to help, but out of manic curiosity to lay eyes on the crimes inside. She hadn't cared one bit for Cecil Tennet – she'd rather wanted to wring his rat nosed neck, but even that didn't make the smell of his insides pleasant when she pulled the shirt aside.

She began to feel cold, her hands shaking just as they had before.

No, she thought. *Don't you let this happen again. You're not helpless! Don't be fuckin helpless, Cadence!*

She fought with the tangles of her wet skirts and rose up. "He was here! Don't let him get away!"

She fought to get the words out, but the cacophony within the bank made her voice sound feeble. A few nearby men glanced her way, frowning and glaring with a strange distaste. She wanted to glare right back, but something about the crowd stilled her usual fury. She felt small there in the wake of the crowd's panic. Instead of scream again, she stepped away from the glaring men just as the doors to the bank burst open. Sheriff Sharples blew past her with a couple deputies in tow, pushing the milling crowd out of the way one at a time. The doors to the bank remained open behind her as several of the ladies fled the place, some accompanied by their husbands.

Cadence stood her ground, calling after the Sheriff as he disappeared into Cecil's office. "He ain't in there! Bell's getting away!"

The Sheriff was too far into the fray to hear her, and again she was met with the disdainful glares.

"What're you lookin at, ya son of a bitch? Get outta my way," she hollered, pushing past the men. She felt weak, but gratefully, they gave way easily. She was disgusted with the morbid desperation of the crowd to get a closer look. The last thing she wanted was to see Cecil Tennet's blood covered face again, but the Sheriff was wasting time. The murderer was getting away.

"Sheriff Sharples!" She called.

Strong arms took hold of her shoulders and pulled her back two steps just as the Sheriff glanced up and met her eyes. His expression changed, but she lost sight of him too quickly to hear his response.

"Come, girl. Come with me," a calm, and strange voice said at her shoulder. She didn't have a chance to look up before she was led out of the bank and into the street.

Outside, crowds were gathering, milling around the windows of the bank and around various women and couples who were weeping or regaling their onlookers with firsthand accounts of the horrors inside. Unlike the saloon, this happened in broad daylight, people were there to see the blood. Sheriff Sharples couldn't simply sweep this under the rug.

"But Packer's in the jail, ain't he?" Someone said in a desperate, hushed voice.

Yet Cadence didn't have time to find the source of the voice as she moved through the muddy streets to the far corner of the bank, still held by those strong hands. She thought to shake free of their hold, but her head was swimming somewhere distant. Cadence could still smell the blood on her clothes, and that smell brought to mind images of things she'd never wished to see again. Cadence wanted to go back, to tell them what she knew, but the look in the Sheriff's eye unnerved her. She let the hands lead her away because there was no fight left in her to give.

They rounded a corner onto a side alley and Cadence finally glanced over her shoulder to see the familiar native man at her shoulder, his expression one of quiet sternness.

She felt an instant of relief – of affection almost, but she destroyed it instantly. Her affections were her greatest betrayal.

She pulled from his hold, and her swooning head knocked her off balance. She leaned hard into the wall of the barber shop. The native man caught her quickly and pushed her forward, this time with a bit more strength. They were moving at an almost frantic pace.

"Stop," she finally said, pulling from his hands again, but he simply ignored her gesture, leading her around another corner into view of a Palomino horse tied up to a nearby tree.

The man let go of her at the horse's shoulder and made quick work of untying the horse's reins. "Get on," he said.

Her eyebrows shot up and fear set in. "No!"

He took hold of her arm and met her gaze. "You must, Cadence. Stop wasting time."

She made to deny his request, but his tone frightened her, and panic began to set in. What choice did she have? She could run from this strange man and cry for help, but the city's population was clamoring to get to the bank. A scream in the midst of this chaos would be lost.

And why would she run from him? He was the only man she knew who'd shown her kindness.

Other than Shannon Bell.

Cadence frowned as she realized she was beginning to think showing her kindness was a tell-tale sign of evil.

"Where are you taking me?" She asked, finally.

"Away. Quickly, damn it!"

She thought to run - but to where? She stepped away from the horse, her tense behavior causing the animal to pin her ears back.

"I don't know you! I ain't goin nowhere -"

The native man lunged toward her, grabbing her elbow as he leaned in close to her. "The city is about to come looking for you, Cadence. They have a witness. Says you murdered the people in the Red Onion."

'What?!" She said, despair tearing through her.

"If we go now, we have a chance. Get on the horse."

She felt her throat grow tight. "But I didn't do anything."

The man tucked something into the saddle bag as he spoke. "Someone came forward. A man named Clairmont? Said he saw you murder three people."

"What?!" She said in a near shriek. "It ain't true!"

"I know!" He hissed. "Get on the horse, damn it. Let me help you!"

Indecision left her stuck there in the mud. There was nowhere to go, no one in the city who harbored affection for her, and the Sheriff's look was not one she wanted to see again.

Cadence realized in this man's words what had unnerved her so about the Sheriff. The look he'd given her – it was suspicion.

She glanced down at her blood soaked dress and felt tears stinging at her eyes. What choice did she have but to go with this stranger? "I don't know you at all. Why would you wanna help me," she said, her lip beginning to tremble.

The native man took the horse's reins in one hand and her hand in the other. "Because I know you didn't do this, and I've unfinished business with the man who did. Now get on the horse. I can't protect you, here."

I can't protect you...

The words were from a stranger, but somehow, she believed him. It wouldn't be the first time he'd been her savior.

This stranger, a man she didn't know at all was the closest thing to a friend she could claim. She stared at the brown and tan patches across the horse's rump, imagining the horrors that might befall her if this man turned out to be bad, too. She'd made the mistake of trusting the wrong man before. What if he led her out into the brush and murdered her, burying her body in some dusty ditch?

"Which way did she go? She can't have gotten far!"

The sound of men hollering startled her around to the alley. The sound was familiar. If it hadn't become a posse yet, it would soon.

"They're coming for you, girl. Get on the horse."

Cadence swallowed and did as she was told, cringing as the bloody mass collected beneath her. Her throat tightened with fear and grief to think she was no longer so much as welcome in the streets of her beloved Cheyenne, but she steadied herself, willing herself brave.

What were the chances of her meeting another murderer so soon? Slim, she hoped. And there was only a chance she'd be murdered by this man in the brush. If she stayed in town, there was no doubt she'd be in the jail or strung up by a mob before sundown.

She'd have to take her chances.

The native man took hold of the horse's mane and a second later was in the saddle in front of her. The sudden surge of movement beneath her knocked her off balance, and she nearly toppled off the back of the horse. The native man reached back, locking his arm behind her as the horse picked up speed. She wrapped her arms around his midsection, forgetting propriety. The horse took off into the trees, the branches whipping against them as they left the chaos and the hollers of Cheyenne behind them.

CHAPTER FOUR

THERE WAS NO TELLING how long they'd been riding before her companion slowed the horse's gait to a walk. The sun was creeping down again toward the west and the cold was beginning to set in. He kept the horse to the outskirts of any ranches they were forced to cross as they headed northwest. They managed to avoid any other travelers or ranch workers, but despite being the only two people for miles, neither of them spoke.

The horse began to huff and shake her mane out in frustration after an hour of easier walking. Without saying a word, the man slid off the side of the horse, took up the reins at the horse's shoulder, and began to lead the creature with Cadence still atop it. He spoke softly to the horse in a language she didn't understand.

Well, that's a good sign, she thought. *Evil men aren't kind to animals. Perhaps he's good.*

Cadence sat atop the horse watching the sun creeping down in the distance. She hadn't brought a shawl or change of clothes. She was not looking forward to bedding down in the brush in blood-soaked rags, but there was no way she'd disrobe to wash and dry them. She'd freeze to death, she was sure.

"Where we goin, anyway?" She asked finally. The cold was giving her the shivers as dusk set in. She hoped a little conversation would distract her from it.

Or was it the memories of her last few days that she wanted a distraction from?

How could anything distract her from that? She was still covered in a dead man's blood.

"Almost there. We'll bed down for the night and be on our way in the morning."

She swallowed. "On our way where?"

He didn't glance up at her. Somewhere during the day, the native man had restored his wide brimmed hat to the top of his head. She couldn't see his face, though he lifted his head to speak. "To wherever Bell might be."

Her chest tightened at the mention of that name. "Why are we following him?"

"The best way to assure you aren't punished for crimes you didn't commit, is to find the man who did, no?"

Cadence let the slow rhythm of the horse's gait rock her hips as she contemplated these words.

What did he intend to do when he found him? Lasso and hog tie him? Drag him all the way back to Cheyenne kicking and screaming? And what was to stop Shannon Bell from rewarding such gumption by cutting this native man's heart out, as well?

She didn't look forward to such an altercation. Not in the least bit.

"Ah, yes. We are here," the man said, pulling the hat from the top of his head. His hair was tied in a braid down his back now, brushing against the blue fabric of his button down shirt. He was dressed in the same kind of clothes a ranch hand or miner might wear. He didn't look native from the neck down, but his face was just as she'd imagined an Indian to be when she was little, watching the neighborhood boys playing Cowboys and Indians. He had a serenity to him that felt out of place after such a long day.

Cadence stared off into the distance to a small group of trees, but she saw nothing but plains in all directions. "We are?"

The man led the horse into the small cluster of trees and tied the creature to a low hanging branch. "You can get down, Miss. We will be bedding down here for the night."

Her stomach sank. She hadn't expected anything less, but still. Seeing the miserable reality of her night's accommodations was enough to make her cry.

She frowned. Was it sleeping in the dirt that would finally break her and make her weep like a woman? How embarrassing.

Cadence was beginning to question the existence of a friendly-faced God smiling down from the heavens.

She let the man help her down off the horse and stretched her legs, feeling pins and needles set in across her backside. Cadence leaned against a tree, watching the man squat down beside the husk of an old trunk. A moment later, he pulled a large satchel from inside and made quick work of unwrapping it.

"Here. Put this on," he said, tossing her a worn, old nightgown.

She furrowed her brow. "Where in the hell'd ya get one of these?"

"Does it matter?"

She supposed not. Still, she couldn't help but wonder if this nightgown belonged to the last woman to ride into the brush with him, and that her body was buried somewhere nearby.

"You can go change behind those trees. When you are done, give me your dress and I'll wash it in the creek."

"I can wash it myself."

He glanced her way, frowning. "I imagine it won't be a pleasant experience. Let me. You warm yourself by the fire."

Before she could ask what fire he referred to, the sharp strike of metal on stone gave sparks from his fingertips, and in an instant, a handful of kindling was ablaze. She hadn't even seen the fire pit upon approach. Apparently, this wasn't his first night in that particular cluster of trees.

Cadence did as he asked, stripping down to her petticoats out of sight. She pulled the nightgown over her head, smelling wood smoke and some earthy, familiar scent beneath that, and returned to the fire, holding the soiled bundle in her arms.

The man spotted her returning and shot up from his perch, his hands out before him. "I'll take that."

"You don't have to do this," she began, but he was already collecting the dress and skirts from her. She watched him, helpless to protest. She didn't have the energy or spirit left to fight anything at that moment. All she wanted in the world was to curl up by that fire and sob.

She'd let herself do at least one of those things.

The man held his hand out to her and led her over the moss and roots of neighboring trees until she was settled down on a fur hide. He quickly gathered up another large fur hide from the hollowed tree and held it out to her, waiting for permission to wrap it around her shoulders.

Why was this stranger being so kind, she wondered? She nodded to him, muttering her gratitude as she pulled the fur around herself.

"The creek is a few yards that way. If you need me, just call."

She swallowed, looking up at his wise face. He wasn't old – perhaps thirties, but his face carried such a calm expression that he felt almost timeless. "Alright," she said, searching for any words that might be worthy of what she was feeling. "What do I call you?"

He smiled at her. "Please, call me Joseph. Now, may I call you Cadence?"

She nodded, almost startled to have someone ask permission.

Joseph took a moment to throw another few pieces of wood onto the fire before disappearing behind the trees.

When he returned, he not only had her clean dress, but also a rabbit dangling long and limp from his left hand.

Her stomach turned. She hadn't eaten in days – the thought of food only conjured the taste of Calvin's blood.

Joseph shot her a sideways glance. "It won't take long."

She frowned. "I'm not very hungry."

He stopped a moment, staring at the ground between them as though he wished to speak. No words came, and he returned his attention to making dinner.

They sat silent a long, both of them staring into the flames as Joseph turned the spit over the fire.

"Thank you," she said, finally.

He glanced up at her, giving barely a nod. "Of course."

The silence continued through his meal, Cadence accepting a small piece of rabbit at his insistence and forcing it down.

Joseph ate slowly, his demeanor that of a monk more than a brave like the ones in the stories she'd heard. When they'd both finished their dinner, Cadence huddled down under her furs and listened to the fire crackling away.

"May I ask how you think we're gonna find him?" She asked.

Joseph startled slightly at this question, his elbow resting on his knee as he idly poked the fire. "Shouldn't be difficult to track him. Wendigoes can't help but leave trails of blood in their wake."

Cadence furrowed her brow, watching him. "Wendigoes?"

Joseph nodded.

She swallowed, almost dreading the answer she'd receive. "What are Wendigoes?"

He took a deep breath, exhaling out his nose as he slumped back against the tree trunk. "A problem."

A long moment passed as she watched him and waited. "That doesn't tell me much," she said finally, frustration playing at her tone.

He opened one eye and shot her a sideways glance. "It is not a pleasant thing. I would think a woman such as yourself would prefer not to know."

"Then you don't know me all that well," she said. She gave each word as much purpose as she could muster, but her heart was tired. She'd traveled a long way, seen horrors she didn't want to relive, and now her only conversation was with a complete stranger. A beautiful stranger, but one whose every word felt like pulling teeth.

Finally, Joseph sat up and began rifling through his leather satchel for something. "This Wendigo is a man with a great sickness. My people know of them."

"He didn't look sick."

"No, but he certainly is."

Cadence let the fur hide slip down her shoulders so Joseph could see her face. "How? How was he sick? Damn it, will ya stop hemmin and hawin over every word? I'm dead tired, I don't have half the mind to deal with this."

Joseph's eyes went wide, but he smiled after a moment, nodding. "I apologize. My people are not accustomed to sharing their stories with white men."

"Well, I ain't a white man, now, am I?" She set her jaw, trying to seem strong, despite feeling as though a stiff breeze might topple her over.

"No, I suppose you are not. Wendigoes are the beasts that eat men."

She shuddered under the hides.

Joseph didn't seem to notice. "They feast on man the way man does on beasts. But unlike men, the Wendigo is never satisfied. The more he eats, the hungrier he becomes. Long ago, you would know a Wendigo to see one. They would grow tall and thin, because with everything they devoured, they would grow larger, leaving them still wanting more. The meal was never enough to still the hunger."

Cadence watched the man's dark eyes, the orange of the flames reflecting there as he spoke. "He didn't look nothing like that," she said.

"He is different. He is a man who has become Wendigo. He has the sickness. He is what he is by choice."

"Why would anyone want to become such a thing?"

Joseph smiled. "Ah, you might be surprised. The curse of Wendigo comes with its blessings."

She scoffed, but he continued.

"See, for every heart the Wendigo devours, he takes on the essence of that man – his strength, his power. That is why many with the sickness seek out the powerful as their victims. The more powerful the man, the more power it gives to the Wendigo."

"Powerful? There weren't nothing powerful about Cal? Damn it, you keep sayin 'man.' Sephy weren't -"

Cadence stopped short, the name catching in her throat. Flashes of Persephone's prone body spilled across the floor of her saloon came flooding to mind. She didn't want to remember these things, but there was no forgetting those fresh sights – the smell of their blood permeating into every surface. The taste -

She swallowed, remembering the slippery feeling of swallowing a piece of Calvin's heart. Her breath stilled in her chest. "How does one become a Wendigo?"

Joseph glanced up at her. "By eating the heart of another man."

Her face contorted against her will and she feared she would weep there by the fire. Despite the stoic distance between them, Joseph lunged up from his seat and came around the fire to be beside her. Clearly, her face had betrayed her. "You are alright, Cadence. You are safe. He won't find you while I'm around."

She shook her head, not wanting to tell him what had happened to her – what his people's stories would say she might become.

The thought of Shannon out there hunting for another victim gave her pause. She glanced over her shoulder toward the edge of the woods, as though Shannon Bell himself would be there, watching them.

Joseph hopped up from beside her and snatched up his satchel. He quickly turned back to her, offering up a leather bundle that smelled of smoked pork. "I know you haven't much of an appetite, but maybe this is more to your tastes?"

She reached out from within her fur confines and snatched it from his hand. Despite the thought of food giving her the shivers for days, she suddenly felt hungry enough to try. She paused, catching him watching her as she tore the leather bundle open and pinched off a piece of jerky. She pressed the dried meat to her tongue and sighed.

"We'll find him, Cadence. And when we do, we'll clear your name. I promise."

Joseph said the words with the certainty of a preacher reciting biblical verse. Then he rolled settled back down across the fire from her, readying himself for sleep.

Cadence watched him a moment, his chest rising and falling as he breathed. She shifted up from the dirt and laid one of the fur hides over him before returning to her own small corner of the camp.

Cadence curled into the confines of the fur's warmth and fought desperately to quiet her mind.

"Just choose a direction."

Cadence looked down at Joseph who stood at the horse's shoulder.

He shot her an almost playful glare. "It's not that simple."

He'd been searching around for almost an hour, poking at the dirt like he'd dropped a penny.

He clucked softly to the horse, a mare he called Thunder, and talked to himself as he mounted, settling in the saddle behind Cadence.

"There are fresh tracks leading off this way. Bit of a cause for concern."

Cadence's brows shot up. "You can't tell me you're sure these random tracks belong to Sha -"

She began to say his name and the sound caught in her throat.

"No, I cannot be sure if they are his, but – they are concerning nonetheless."

Cadence glanced down at the grass, searching the earth for any sign of what Joseph could see.

"Why? What's wrong with them?"

Joseph tugged on the reins, turning the horse toward hills in the west. "They're heading toward the Indian Agency."

"So?"

"So, there are few reasons for any man from Cheyenne to be heading there."

Before Cadence could press further, Joseph gave the horse a kick and they were off.

She fought to straighten her back, not wanting to press against his chest. There was an unavoidable intimacy to him seated there behind her, even more so than the day before when he rode on the front. She leaned toward the horse's head as they began to trudge down the hill.

She managed to get a few details from her stoic companion, including the distance to the agency.

"A day's ride?" She said, practically sighing in misery.

Suppose you should get used to it. It's not like you've got a bed to sleep in anymore. Probably won't again for a very long time.

Unless they arrest you. They have beds in the jails, she thought.

His arm slid around her middle just as the horse huffed in frustration. He'd pulled her back against him before she could protest. "Mustn't lean forward. Will cause the horse to struggle."

She sat stone still, feeling Joseph's chest against her back, feeling his thighs at her hips. She hadn't been this close to a man since Shannon, or perhaps even Goldrup. It felt strange to be held so close without the promise of intimacy.

Joseph released his hold on her and she exhaled, only then realizing she'd been holding her breath. He let his arms rest across her hips, holding the reins against her stomach.

They rode at an easier pace, the fear of chasing mobs having receded. Still, Joseph glanced over his shoulder more than she liked. There was no sign of horses kicking up dust on the horizon, nor the sound of pitchforks and spades clanging together in the distance. Just the sound of the birds and the grass flitting around in the breeze. Still, he kept glancing back, making her half nervous at the notion of what else might be there – or who.

When she followed his gaze, there was nothing to see, but the plains.

They made it within miles of a small cluster of buildings and houses just before sundown. Joseph explained that these chimneyed structures were the Indian Agency, but he chose not to ride closer. Instead, he tied the horse up to a tree and settled Cadence in with a fire and her warm hides.

"I'm going to ride ahead and see if this will be a welcome place. Will you be alright to wait?"

Her stomach turned at the thought of being completely alone. What if he didn't come back? What if he left her there with no horse and no notion of where she was? She may have served a good number of Indians in the Red Onion, but the people in the village below didn't know that. What reason would they have to welcome her?

Memories of playing Cowboys and Indians as a child came to mind. She scolded herself for even contemplating the people living in the distance might scalp her.

She began to protest his leaving, but he stopped her, handing her his leather bundle of smoked pork.

"It is only three miles on from here, I believe. You can see it from the hilltop. It will take me only an hour, maybe two."

"Why can't I just go along with you? They might have rooms, maybe? A real bed to sleep in. I could work for lodgin if they let me," she said, her words spilling out over each other as she realized what little she had to offer on her own.

In the decade since her Mama died, she'd never felt so helpless as she did at that moment. She'd been forced to pretend the saloon was Cal's, pretend she was his employee, pretend she wasn't in charge – all because she was a woman. Now, the notion of offering work in exchange for anything was limited to begging, selling her body, or helping on a ranch taking care of some rich folks' meals and kids. There weren't many options for a woman this far into the middle of nowhere.

She didn't imagine there were too many rich folks living on the Indian lands, either.

"Word travels fast. I need to be sure it is safe for you - us."

He wouldn't budge on his decision, untying the horse and heading off just after making sure she'd eaten some of the pork jerky. Cadence sat there under the trees, cuddling up in the fur hides as much to hide from being seen as to keep warm.

An hour passed with little more of note than the sound of critters scurrying and chirping in the grass. The air was crisp, and each breeze only inspired her to bundle deeper into her hides. She kept her eyes cast downhill, watching for a sign of Joseph's return and willing the unfortunate thoughts of being left there to fend for herself out of mind.

Smoke began to turn a dark color as the fires in the outpost were fed in the early evening. Cadence pulled out the small leather satchel Joseph left for her and took another small bite of jerky. She gnawed it between her molars, growing thirstier with every passing moment. Another hour passed and there was still no sign of Joseph. Cadence made a conscious choice to be irritated with him. Irritation felt safer than fear.

Irritation was the response to him running late.

Fear was the response to him never coming back at all.

Her thirst began to get the best of her after finishing off the small bundle of jerky, and she rose from her furry perch, turning toward the open grasses. The river was just a hundred yards off – cool running water, more than she could ever drink.

She stood a moment, contemplating the distance. She'd still be able to see Joseph climbing the hill toward her perch from down that slope, wouldn't she?

Another ten minutes passed, and she decided she didn't care. If he returned to find her post in disarray and her gone, it would be his turn to worry. If worry would be the response to finding he no longer had to fend for this silly white woman who was surely more trouble to him than she was worth.

Cadence marched down the hillside, feeling the grass flit against her bare legs. Her stockings had been bloodstained enough that she didn't want to wear them another day. They were balled up in an empty tree trunk a day's ride back toward Cheyenne. It felt almost thrilling roaming the world with bare legs. She imagined the hoots and hollers of her patrons back at the Red Onion were she to show a little bare ankle.

Then she frowned, shaking her head to cast off these thoughts. There was little left she could dwell on that didn't make her miserable.

She approached the river, seeing the expanse of it fully for the first time. It was a good twenty or thirty meters wide there, and flowing clear over thousands of smooth stones, all glistening just under the surface. Cadence dropped down to the water, scooped her hands into the frigid depths and brought a mouthful of water to her lips. She sighed loudly as the cold liquid settled into her stomach. She knelt there a moment, resting back on her ankles as a nice breeze kicked up, casting tiny ripples across the water.

She leaned forward to take another drink just as the sound of horses clamoring over the plains caught her attention. She straightened, turning back toward the East and the direction of the sound. The group wasn't visible yet, but they were coming her way at quite a clip.

Her stomach turned. She shifted, setting one foot under her to rise and greet whatever came her way. The knot she got in her stomach around strange men wouldn't stop her from holding her head high when they approached.

The water took her breath away as some immense force slammed into her back and charged her full steam into the water. She flailed against it, but the sensation of arms wrapping around her waist was barely noticeable in the wake of the cold. She gasped for air with every step deeper. Soon the water was up to her belly, and she could barely breathe from the shock of cold. She clutched at the hand that held her, pulling at each finger to free herself. They were chest deep before she managed to catch her breath enough to scream. Another hand clamped over her mouth just as the riders came into view in the distance. She flung her arms in the air to get their attention, but it was too late. An instant later, her captor plunged her head under the water, holding her there as the gentle rapids swirled her blonde hair across her face.

She struggled against his hold, swinging her arms in the water as though she might hit her assailant, but his hold was too strong, and the cold shocked the last of her breath from her lungs. She was going to drown there, miles away from everyone and everything familiar, no one to know her name but Joseph. Joseph, the man who'd abandoned her there on the hillside to be drowned by some mad plainsman. She curled her fingers into the soaked fabric of the man's shirt and pulled, feeling it tear in her hands.

The open air hit her face and she gasped so desperately it sounded like a dying animal. She jerked away, yanking herself free of the man's loosened grip and turned, ready to fight this lunatic that seemed so hell bent on seeing her drown.

"You're ok, Cadence. Just breathe."

She jumped even further at the sound of the voice with almost as much fervor as she had the frozen water. She spun around to find Shannon Bell standing up to his chest in the river, his dark hair soaked and clinging to his face and neck.

Cadence scrambled backward to get away from him, losing her footing on the rocky riverbed as she used what little breath she had to scream anew. He looked different now. He wasn't the man in black anymore. The bounty hunter was gone now. Instead, he wore brown britches, a green shirt with the sleeves rolled up, and navy suspenders. He looked like a ranch hand or a farmer. Wholesome, almost.

Everything about him seemed different save for soft look in his eyes.

"Cadence, sh! They'll hear you."

She turned, fighting to move through the water, cursing her parents for never teaching her to swim. She was moving toward the riverbed achingly slow, her skirts pulling her downriver with the current. His arms were at her side again, holding her by the waist.

He was going to try drowning her again.

"Please! Don't hurt me! I won't tell anyone! I won't say anything!" She cried, her voice wavering with each word.

"What?" He said, and his tone stilled her a moment. "Cadence, I would never hurt you."

He let go of her waist, and she fell into the shallow water, the stones jutting up into her backside. She turned up to find him standing over her, a pained expression on his face.

"You tried to drown me," she said, panting between the words.

He ran his fingers up through his wet hair, pushing it out of his face, then wiped his hand over his eyes. "Woman, why won't you believe me, damn it? I'm not going to hurt you."

"Right! I've seen what you do!" She demanded, kicking her foot into the water to splash at him as she screamed again.

He dropped to a squat beside her. "Those riders – they were lookin for you. They're from Cheyenne. I couldn't let 'em see you."

Cadence frowned, staring up at Shannon's now gentle looking face. This ranch hand version of him felt like a normal fellow – almost. He still felt like leaning over a bonfire.

"You God damn snake! You think I'm going to believe you after you sneak up on me -"

"Would you have let me come close had you seen me?"

She kicked her foot in the water again, crawling away. "No!"

She caught sight of his face. The murdering bastard was giving her a sarcastic glare. "Well, there you have it."

She lay there panting, afraid to stand up and run from him. She felt like a child in the sights of a rabid dog – a beast simply waiting for an invitation to attack and kill. They both remained there a moment in silence. Finally, Cadence shifted on the rocky ground and rolled over to stand up.

Shannon reached for her, and she shrieked, lunging away from him. Her wet skirts caught around her legs, and she lost footing, landing with a hard thud on her hip.

"Come now, Duchess. I'm not going to hurt you."

She stood, watching him, backing up onto the riverbed. "You're here because you're hungry then, yeah? Is that what happens now? You're here to tear my heart out and eat it." Her voice was shaking with fear, and the sound of it made her so angry, she could spit fire. "You ain't gonna get much power from me, but you go right ahead! I ain't got nothing else to -"

"What nonsense have you -"

"Wendigo? Ain't that what they call you? Eater of men. Persephone weren't no man, Shannon! You fuckin monster!"

Shannon lunged at her, grabbing her by the shoulders. "I didn't do those things, Cadence. Look at me!"

"No," she screamed, shaking in his grasp as she tried to free herself. His grip was too strong; he wouldn't let her go.

"Listen to me. I didn't hurt your kin, woman! I didn't fucking do this!"

"Liar. You can't take back what you did to me. You can't take back what you made me do!"

Shannon stared at her a moment, his grip loosening. She glared right back, remembering the taste of Calvin's blood.

Shannon's eyes softened. "No, I can't. And I'm sorry, but what I did, I did for you."

"You son of a bitch!" She screamed, her voice cracking with tears. Still, she managed to hold them in.

Her mouth fell open, but she couldn't find the words to speak. How could he proclaim his innocence of one crime in a breath, then declare pride for another in the next? "How can you say that?"

Shannon turned toward the West, collecting a jacket and hat from the ground as he went. "Get to cover, Cadence. Stay out of sight, alright?"

"Answer me, damn it! How can you say that? If you're not a monster -"

He turned back, swatting his hat through the air as though he could knock her words down. "You don't know what I know, Cadence. If you did - I may be sorry, but I wouldn't take it back if I could."

He stood there watching her for a long moment, but she didn't move. She stared at his dark eyes, waiting for him to turn on her.

"Are you what he says you are?" She asked finally, breaking the heavy silence.

He closed his eyes and took a deep breath. "Yes," he said, and it was as though the air all but disappeared. "But I'm no monster."

With that, Shannon turned and marched off toward the Indian Agency, his soaked clothes clinging to every inch of him. "Stay out of sight."

Then he was gone beyond the crest of the hill, and Cadence stood alone, her body growing colder with each passing breeze.

CHAPTER FIVE

"WHAT HAPPENED TO YOU?" Joseph asked when he finally returned from the Agency.

Cadence was huddled under the furs, shivering. She hadn't dared take off the dress to hang it for fear Joseph, Shannon, or a gaggle of horse riding bounty hunters might stumble upon her and find her in her pantaloons.

She fought with her own mind.

She struggled to speak. "Fell in the river."

He stared at her a long moment, pulling his wide-brimmed hat from atop his head. She felt small in his gaze.

Why wasn't she telling him the truth? That the man he was hunting had dragged her into the water and held her under. Why wasn't she blurting out his name – *Shannon Bell was here! He was here, he tried to drown me, and now he's down at the agency doing God knows what! Let's get him!*

Instead, she was letting Joseph think she was an imbecile.

"What were you doing in the river?"

She stared off toward the trails of chimney smoke in the distance, watching them crawl their way up into the clouds. "I was thirsty."

"I see," he said after a pause. Joseph then dropped to his knees nearby. "Well here, let me get the fire going a little higher to warm you up, then I'll go refill your canteen and cook us some supper."

Cadence watched him stirring the fire. She could still feel her heart pounding in her chest, found herself glancing over her shoulder for Shannon every few minutes.

She should be terrified, shouldn't she?

Joseph pulled a still feathered bird from his satchel, then mischievously admitted to stealing the chicken on his way out of town. "It isn't my fault the agents didn't want to do business with a red man off the reservation."

Cadence watched him, the shivering subsiding now with the roaring fire before her.

The two of them settled in to eat their supper, Cadence did her best to eat with him, silently wishing she hadn't eaten all of the smoked jerky he left her. She ate until she finally felt warm enough to curl up for the night.

She was still on constant watch for Shannon, but as Joseph sat across the fire from her whittling a piece of wood with his knife, she felt safe enough to close her eyes.

Sleep came in fits at first, waking with a start every few moments to be sure she hadn't rolled into the fire or that Joseph was still holding his peaceful watch.

Finally, Cadence began to dream. She was walking through tall grasses, feeling their blades in her fingers as she passed. But this plain wasn't like the others she'd seen. This one had no end in sight. The grass grew high and wild in every direction, as far as the sky, and as she knew in her heart, further. She was lost in a sea of nothing, one with nowhere, and she was terrified.

The wind picked up and suddenly she could hear a familiar sound. Riders were coming in the distance. She stood there frozen, afraid to meet the coming horde. Were they friend or foe, she didn't know, but she was half ready to accept the fate of a lynch mob or a jail. Four walls sounded safer than the endlessness.

She stood her ground, awaiting the incoming riders when suddenly a smell caught her off-guard. She spun around, searching for the source.

It was everywhere.

The landscape had changed. In every direction, the grass was now weighed down with blood. The world was red around her, dripping from the blades of grass as though it had rained from the heavens. She cried out, feeling her feet sink into the sticky warmth of it. It was rising. Like the river had overwhelmed her that day, now this sea of blood was gathering around her, creeping up her legs. She could feel the trickle of it beneath her, moving against her skin until it was at her sex.

Cadence's eyes burst open, and she sat up in the dark. The fire was burned down now, and Joseph was sound asleep on the other side of the camp. She was grateful to be alone at that moment.

Cadence's face contorted in horror as she pressed her hands down to her skirts, pulling them up. There was blood everywhere. Her skirts, her pantaloons, the fur hides that had kept her warm – Joseph's fur hides – all of it was covered in blood. Her blood.

She froze.

Cadence's mind raced with everything she *should* do – quietly make her way to the river, clean herself up, hide all evidence of her accident.

Yet as she took in the sight of all that red, Cadence could do nothing, but stifle tears. Her first thought at the sight of the blood had been of Shannon – that he'd come back. That she'd kept him a secret from Joseph, and he'd come back to hurt her.

This wasn't the first time her monthly had surprised her in the night, but something had changed in Cadence. The smell and sight of the blood shot a familiar knot into her throat that she couldn't swallow. This blood was innocent, but she couldn't fight the panic. It was as though her body had betrayed her, forcing her to see the horrors of the Red Onion all over again.

But above that, she was in the middle of nowhere, surrounded by nothing, her only companion a strange man she hardly knew, and there was no way to still the blood. She didn't have her linens to tie under her pantaloons, nor a bathtub or a basin to clean herself or her clothes. She was a mess, the furs were a mess, and the memories of fear flooding back left her helpless and useless, just staring at her hands as tears streamed down her face.

She couldn't move. If she couldn't move, he would see. Joseph would see.

Cadence looked at her fingers, now covered in her blood, and she sobbed.

"Miss Cadence," Joseph said, softly. "Are you alright?"

Her tears came now with twice the force. The strange man was awake. He would know what had happened to her and the shame of it ruptured in her chest. She turned her face away and sobbed harder.

"Please don't look at me," she said, barely managing to get the words out.

Joseph was beside her in an instant, looking her over with rampant concern. "Are you injured? How were you hurt?"

His gentle response only upset her further and she began to bawl uncontrollably, scrambling to get away from him, and from the memories of the Red Onion.

She'd kept tears at bay in the days since the murders, but now as she lay huddled in the dirt under some godforsaken tree, the grief of everything hit her like hangman's noose.

She couldn't fight the panic, she was going to die there in the brush.

"He was here," she whispered, wanting to share her fear with Joseph so that he might protect her.

"What?"

"He was -" She stopped, stilling the words before she could confess herself. What would he think of her if he knew she'd protected a murderer? She couldn't tell him. She might lose him, too.

Joseph leaned over her, his dark brown eyes heavy with concern and worry. He kept glancing at her hands, touching his own to her belly and her face, trying to quiet her sobs long enough to know what was wrong.

"Cadence, where are you bleeding from?"

Joseph reached for her, pulling the hides away only to find her blood on his hands. Cadence recoiled as Joseph's concerned face looked puzzled for a moment.

He was at her side again, his voice as gentle as though he spoke to a spooked horse. "Come now, Cadence. You're alright. Come here, creature."

His arms moved around her, and she flailed against the touch, curling into herself as she felt more blood spilling from its source. He did not let her loose his hold and instead lifted her up from the ground cradling her in his arms.

"No! No," she cried. "Put me down."

Joseph ignored her protests and carried her out from the trees, sauntering with an easy gait down the hillside. Despite the weight of her, he moved as though she were as light as a small child. She couldn't hold onto him or fight him, her hands were bloody and she didn't dare get it on him. She turned her face away as far as she could, feeling his breath in her hair as they reached the riverbed. Instead of stopping, Joseph marched right into the water until he was waist deep.

"Here we are. It's cold, but it will soothe you."

He slowly lowered her legs down into the water and the shock of the cold stopped her tears in her throat. She felt the stony surface under her feet and straightened, feeling the water flood between her legs, lifting her skirts in a billow around her. Joseph took her by the shoulders and turned her to face him. She could not meet his gaze, keeping her head turned as Joseph took her hands in his and began to wash them in the cold water, still cooing softly to her in whispered words.

"You're safe," he said. "There's no one here, but us. You're safe."

A sob caught in her throat. These words were a lie. Shannon could be close by, and she'd kept that from him. Men on horseback – a lynch mob – could be close by, and she hadn't said a word for fear of having to explain how they hadn't seen her.

She let his strong hands move between her fingers, scrubbing them of any sign of blood. Then before she could protest, Joseph took hold of the ties at her dress. She startled, meeting his eyes for the first time.

His eyebrows shot up, but his expression was still one of cautious calm. "Don't look down. Look at the stars."

She did as she was told, focusing on one twinkling corner of the black to another, stifling sobs as Joseph helped her out of her bloody dress. A moment later she stood there in her pantaloons and undergarments as Joseph roughly scrubbed the fabric together out of sight. She could hear him lifting the garment from the water to inspect it between each scrub. She pressed her hands to the front of her corset and closed her eyes, willing her chin to stop trembling. Yet, the fear and panic were subsiding. Even the shame was almost fading away as both emotions were overwhelmed by gratitude and humility. This man she hardly knew – a man whose kind Calvin had refused service more than once when he first took over the Red Onion - was being kinder to her than even her mother had the very first time she'd bled as a woman. How could a man be this kind? How was he not appalled?

"Here," he said suddenly, startling her eyes open. He held her petticoat up to her. There wasn't a speck of red upon it. She took it in her shaking hands. The cold had left her thighs completely numb, and with each breeze, the air began to feel colder than the water. Cadence sank down lower and finally let herself look down. There were no billowing clouds of red around her, at least not anymore, and as she pulled her petticoat back on, she rustled her hand into the fabric between her legs, hoping to bat away any blood that might linger there. She didn't dare take them off. Not with Joseph standing so close.

"Let me help you," Joseph said, holding the soaking dress open for her to step in. She obliged him, and for the first few moments, the dress retained the water's temperature, feeling almost warm in the cold air. That soon changed and she was shivering violently by the time they reached their camp.

Cadence fought to still her tears, but they continued. Joseph gave the fire a quick stir and helped her settle down next to the flames. Still, she could not stop crying.

"What is wrong?" He asked finally. "Do you not feel well?"

Cadence shook her head, but a sob snuck out in response. She didn't want to admit the embarrassment she felt, or that even with all the kindness he'd just shown her, she didn't have any of her linens to tie under her petticoats, and she would bleed through them every day – multiple times a day – until the bleeding stopped. She'd only humiliate herself again on an hourly basis, but next time they might not be near a river for her to wash.

And atop all of that, her greatest embarrassment was that she'd kept secrets from this man – the kindest human being she'd ever met.

"You are not ashamed, are you?"

"I am," she said, her lip curling with the admittance. In more ways than one, she thought.

Joseph made a gentle scoffing sound. "In my tribe, the medicine women spoke of a woman's time of the moon as a powerful time."

"What?" Cadence managed to eke out the word without sniffling.

"The moon time. It is when a woman bleeds," he said, gesturing to her. Cadence's cheeks burned. Joseph glanced up at the sky and smiled. "Your time is during the absent moon. That's a powerful time. You'd make good medicine now."

She furrowed her brow, unable to receive some strange compliment from the man who'd just spent twenty minutes washing her drawers. "Ain't feelin too powerful," she said, and the tears returned.

Joseph crawled across the camp to her and settled at her side, touching his hand to her head in an awkward attempt to comfort. "What can I do?"

She frowned at him, fighting to make a joke through her tears. "You could buy back my saloon for me. It'd be nice to have my things right now. Or even a bath -"

Cadence's face contorted and she pressed her hands over her eyes. She'd never felt so fragile in her life, and she hated it. Yet by some curse, everything she'd been through, everything she would go through – all of it felt too heavy to bear suddenly in the knowledge that she might never get to have her own bathtub, or her own change of dresses, or her own linens ever again.

Joseph stared at her for a long moment, then rose to his feet, moving across the camp. She watched him when instead of settling in to bed down again as she expected him to, Joseph packed up his things, his bloodied furs, and his satchel and loaded it all up onto his horse. He then snuffed out the last of the coals in their fire and held his hand out to her.

"What are you doing?" She asked.

She took his hand, and without a word, he piled her up on the horse and rode hastily down the hilly landscape toward the agency.

"Wait! What about those men from Cheyenne? Won't they be lookin for me?"

Joseph glanced over his shoulder at her, his brow furrowed as the horse tottered along beneath them. "No. They were just passing through on their way to Palmer Outpost. How did you know about them?"

She held her arms around his belly, feeling his muscles shift as the horse moved down the hill. Cadence paused. "I saw em when I was down by the river. They came hootin through. It's why I fell in."

Joseph shook his head, chuckling softly to himself. "No need to worry yourself. They're long gone. And you'll sleep in a bed tonight."

Cadence swallowed, watching the run down village growing larger as they approached. There was someone else in the Indian Agency she was afraid to see. Still, she rode along with Joseph as silent as the night around them.

"Here you are, sweetheart. This should be your size."

The woman held the green dress out to Cadence, flashing her a smile of startlingly white teeth. Cadence took the garment, feeling the snug pressure of her linens tied tightly beneath her pantaloons. She was dry now, well rested, and bathed, and the woman that stood before her was almost as kind as her Joseph.

The woman introduced herself as Beatrice the night before when she'd let Cadence into her small home to sleep on a cot by the fire. Joseph had disappeared, happy to bed down in the brush again for the night. Cadence tried to protest, but the matronly woman would hear none of it as she herded Cadence in toward the fire and set her to bed for the night.

The agency smelled oddly familiar as Cadence dressed that morning. The fabric of her new dress smelled smoky and warm, the off white fabric of her new linens were stiff from having never been worn before.

She felt new as she stepped out of Beatrice's small home early that morning, taking in the dower mood of the place.

Despite Beatrice's kind smile, no other part of the Indian Agency felt warm. Men and women were living in these small houses, some with children, others too old to have such. Many of them wore clothes like herself and Joseph, but Cadence spotted an older man at the window of one of the houses, his clothes made of tanned hides. Cadence stepped out into the main roadway of the agency, hearing the distant sound of children. She thanked Beatrice and headed out to find her companion, walking up the center of the agency with as confident a gait as she could muster.

Each dark face that peered from the window or stared from their front steps seemed to watch her with open suspicion. She had no place there. The only other white people she'd seen were an officer posted at the far end of the village and a proprietor of a small trading post who handed out small brown bottles to the older Indian men who came to his window.

There was no sign of Shannon, and from the looks of the dark faces she met, she was certainly the only unfamiliar white face to be found in the agency that morning.

Cadence glanced between each house, searching for a familiar face as the sound of children grew louder. She rounded the corner of the trading post and spotted a dusty schoolhouse, several tiny people running about just outside. The sight of the children made her smile. The girls had long braids of black hair down their backs like Joseph, but the two young boys had short shorn hair. It looked almost strange to see an Indian without his hair. She'd never seen such a thing before.

Cadence passed the small schoolhouse, smiling to the children outside when they shot her quizzical looks. One of the little girls smiled and waved back to her, but the young boys simply stared.

She passed the schoolhouse and reached the open space of the plains beyond, scanning the horizon for a sign of Joseph's camp. There were no trees to be seen, nothing to offer him the cover he preferred for setting up camp. Cadence turned to walk to the far end of the agency when a little girl darted past her into the fields.

This little girl's hair was loose, flitting in long waves of black behind her as she barreled past, her gray dress catching in the tall grass.

Cadence glanced back toward the school, but there was no sign of the other children now. School had begun.

Cadence watched the little girl a moment as the tiny thing stopped in the grass and dropped to the ground, disappearing entirely from view. Cadence couldn't help but laugh.

"Hey there, little lady," Cadence called as she approached the small girl's hiding place. The little girl popped her head up, her eyes wide with conspiracy, and pressed her finger to her lips. Cadence ducked down into the grass, chuckling softly as she crawled over to sit by the girl.

"Are we skipping school today, little miss?"

The girl shot her a sideways look, her dark eyes betraying wisdom well beyond her few years. The girl looked to be no older than seven years old, her hair as wild as the grass around them.

"Sh! Ms. George will hear you!" The girl hissed.

"Oh, well we wouldn't want that."

The girl smiled at her, but the smile disappeared instantly when a stern voice called across the plain.

"Not again, you little brat!"

Cadence's stomach lurched at the teacher's tone. She took a deep breath and gave the little girl a sad, resigned look. "I think your teacher is looking for you."

The girl frowned up at Cadence, then with an air of almost regal grace, stood from her hiding space, dusting the front of her dress as she did. Cadence rose to her feet beside the little girl and at once felt tiny fingers intertwining with her own. Cadence squeezed the girl's hand, and they stepped out from the grass to make their way back toward the school.

"I told you what would happen if you played these games again, girl."

The teacher was a tall, thin, white woman with almost gaunt features and a massive bun of dirty blonde hair atop her head. Cadence walked with the girl to meet the teacher, but when Ms. George reached for the child, Cadence held tight to her hand.

The teacher glared down at the girl, tapping her foot impatiently. "Well, you best move quickly."

The girl didn't let go of Cadence's hand. Cadence dropped to her knees beside the girl, brushing a long wisp of black hair behind the girl's ear. "What's your name, beautiful?"

The girl opened her mouth but took a moment to speak. "It's – They made me choose Margaret, but that's not my real name."

Cadence frowned. "Who made you choose a name?"

The little girl looked up at Ms. George who simply rolled her eyes.

"Well, what was the name your Momma gave you?" Cadence asked.

The girl's eyes brightened. "Not my Momma, but my chief named me -"

"Don't you dare, Margaret."

Cadence grew wary at the teacher's tone but fought to hide it from the little girl. "It's alright, Ms. George. I would like to hear it."

Ms. George glared at her. "No, it is not alright -"

"My name is -"

"If you say one more word, Margaret, you will get the cane again. You wouldn't want that two days in a row, now, would you? What would the other children think?"

The girl's eyes fell, and Cadence's heart ached. She touched her hands to the girl's shoulders and squeezed gently, wanting desperately to share a loving touch with the child – to soothe the brutality of this teacher's threats.

"My name is Margaret," the girl said, tears welling up in her eyes.

Rage rose in Cadence's chest, but she kept her voice as calm as she could.

"See. My Momma named me Cadence. There's a lotta people say that's a man's name, so a lot of people try to call me Cady. I don't like that very much," Cadence paused, turning to look up at the teacher. "- because that isn't my name. Do you feel like that, too?"

The girl nodded, wiping tears away from her eyes.

"Well then, I don't want to call you anything, but what your Momma named you. You can tell me. I want you to."

The girl took a shaky breath, opened her mouth, and Ms. George lunged forward, squeezing her bony fingers around the little girl's forearm. "Don't you dare -"

Cadence turned toward the teacher, seething. "You will let her tell me her name, Miss George."

Ms. George's hands dropped at her side and her face went slack with shock. Something had happened. Something wrong.

Ms. George stared at Cadence with her mouth open, as though she were fighting to speak and couldn't. Cadence stared back at the woman as the little girl finally found her voice.

"My name is Chenoa."

Cadence's heart broke. The name was so beautiful, and so completely suited to the little girl. No word had ever sounded so natural on a person's lips.

Cadence fought to keep the smile on her face. "Well, it is very nice to meet you, Chenoa. You have a truly beautiful name."

Ms. George reached for Chenoa, clutching her arm tight enough to cause the girl to flinch, and pulled her toward the school. Cadence rose to her full height beside Ms. George. She was not as tall as the lithe woman, but Cadence sensed Ms. George's demeanor was different now.

Cadence knew exactly how Miss George felt and seeing the terror in the woman's eyes brought Cadence a fleeting sense of satisfaction. Cadence stepped toward the stern teacher and met her eyes. "You will never call this girl 'Margaret' again, do you understand?"

Ms. George's eyes went wide, but she didn't speak.

"And you will never hit or abuse any of these children ever again. You will be kind. You will be patient."

The woman choked back a sob as her eyes flickered with fear. Cadence felt her heart pounding in her chest. This was what Joseph spoke of –this was the power she possessed, and Ms. George was helpless to any command Cadence might give. She felt dizzy in its magnitude.

"You will throw that cane in the fire tonight, and you will call all of these children by their true names."

Chenoa stared up from Ms. George's side, a look of awe on her face as Miss George finally swallowed and nodded at Cadence.

"You are free to go. Enjoy your day, Chenoa. If you do all your school work you can grow up to be a teacher, too."

Ms. George began to lead the little girl away, gently.

"I don't want to be a teacher," Chenoa called back. "I'm gonna be a chief!"

Cadence smiled wide, waving to the girl and watched Chenoa disappear into the rickety building, several of the other children peering out from the open door as she went.

Cadence waited until the door was shut before wiping the tears from her eyes.

She finally found Joseph standing outside Beatrice's house. He'd come to collect her while she was out searching for him. He stood by the door to Beatrice's home, Thunder's saddlebags filled to bursting with her now dry and freshly washed clothes from the night before.

"Are you well enough to travel?" He asked as she approached. His expression betrayed concern and she pressed her hand to her face. Her eyes betrayed her crying again.

Cadence shook it off as best she could. "I am. Where will we go now?"

Beatrice handed a small bundle to Joseph, nodding to him in such a way that Cadence stopped.

She waited for Beatrice to meet her gaze and smiled. "Thank you so much, ma'am."

Beatrice just smiled right back. "Don't you worry yourself. Any friend of Joseph is welcome here."

With that, she turned back and disappeared into her house.

Cadence turned to Joseph who was already mounting their horse. He glanced down at her, holding out his hand to help her up. When she didn't take it, he raised his eyebrows.

"We're following the trail to Palmer. It's our best bet right now," he said, as though he needed to convince her to keep him company. He offered a smile, causing his brown eyes to light up. Cadence remembered the morning outside the Cheyenne jail, when Joseph's face was fully visible to her for the first time. He'd almost knocked the wind right out of her.

Cadence remembered it clearly as his smile almost keeled her over.

Cadence stood there a long moment, contemplating the past day. Should she tell him Shannon had come through? Would he be angry that she'd kept it until now?

Would he ever smile at her like that again if he knew?

She nodded and let Joseph help her climb onto the horse.

They rode through the small village, dark faces peering out from their windows at her as they passed. When they trotted past the small schoolhouse, a familiar little smile appeared in one of the windows, her wild hair now braided down her shoulder.

Cadence felt a gentle thrill at the memory of Ms. George's terrified face and waved back to little Chenoa before they broke into a canter and rode off into the plains.

The hills to the west betrayed more tree cover, and Joseph tied his horse to a shaded clearing before setting to the work of building a fire. He'd made a point to settle them near a creek bed for Cadence to wash her linens and left her to the work while he searched for firewood. Cadence gratefully pulled the fresh bundle of linens from one of Joseph's saddlebags and headed down to the creek to wash the first set. She felt lighter there, suddenly. The shade of the trees, the cool air quieter than anything she'd ever felt before. They hadn't spoken much that day, Cadence content to dwell in the silence of her own thoughts, but now that they were camped for the night, she had questions. She had a wave of curiosity rising that wanted to be sated. Once she was done washing and redressing, she hung her wet linens from a tree branch and plopped down by the fire.

She watched Joseph move about the camp, beating out the furs before laying them on the ground beside her. He tossed her a small leather bundle of jerky to snack on – the same bundle Beatrice offered him that morning. She unwrapped the meat and took a small pinch. Her mouth salivated just at the sight of the bundle. There was something about it – the seasoning or manner in which it was smoked – that made it delectable in a way nothing else was. It made her thirsty afterward, but still too delicious to refuse. She wrapped it back up and set it aside. She didn't want to eat too much if Joseph didn't have any luck finding something for supper.

"You're rather quiet today," he said, finally.

Cadence pretended to be surprised by this comment. She'd been lost in her thoughts all day. She'd kept Shannon's presence a secret, she'd been both mortified the night before and amazed by kindness.

But the events of that morning overshadowed all these other thoughts.

She'd stilled that woman with just a word. She'd torn Ms. George's free will from her and replaced her brutality with a very tight leash. Cadence wondered how long the compulsion would last. Would Miss George be a gentler woman toward those children forever or would it fade with time?

Cadence wanted to know. She wanted to test it again, to see how powerful she truly was.

Joseph slumped down into his seat across the fire from her, his wide brimmed hat still settled atop his head. She watched him for a long moment, contemplating whether or not compelling this new friend would be wrong. It would just be a test – the simplest of requests.

Still, if he could feel what she was doing, would he feel betrayed? Would he ever trust her again?

"Are you alright?" He asked, finally.

"Give me your hat," she said, watching him closely.

He shot her a raised eyebrow from beneath the brim of his hat. Then with a half chuckle, he pulled the hat off his head and tossed it over the fire to her. "Not sure it's quite your style but have at it."

Cadence caught the hat, holding it in her hands as her brow furrowed. Yes, he'd done as she asked, but it didn't feel the same. His handing over the hat had been a choice. He wasn't compelled – he wasn't helpless to the demand. He simply thought it silly and agreed.

Cadence slumped back into her seat.

Why didn't it work on Joseph?

She sighed. Shannon had power over her when they first met, but Joseph was unaffected. Was she just not powerful enough? Was it because Joseph was a man?

There was no knowing, she realized. The only person who could know the answers she sought was Shannon and Shannon wasn't there to answer.

And Shannon was a murderer.

Cadence held the hat for a long moment, feeling silly. She finally handed it back and joined Joseph in staring at the fire.

They passed the time in silence, Joseph returning his attention to whittling the same piece of wood he'd been toying with for a few nights. Cadence watched him until a soft rustle startled them both toward the deeper woods.

Joseph hopped up excitedly. "Cross your fingers!"

He disappeared into the trees, and after a long moment, returned with another rabbit hanging limply from his hand.

"How do you do that?" She asked, honestly in awe.

He smiled. "It's just setting the snare and being patient. I can teach you if you like."

Cadence nodded. "I think I'd like that."

Joseph smiled, dropping to his knees just outside the camp to strip the rabbit. She watched his shoulders, the long braid swaying with every tiny movement of his arms.

When he finally returned, the rabbit skewered on a long spit, Cadence watched Joseph's face and asked one of the hundred questions she had on her mind.

"What's your real name?"

His eyebrows shot up and he chuckled, softly. "Why would you want to know that?"

"I just do."

He gave an almost surprised smile. "My apologies. Most white folk prefer my Christian name. I am called -"

Sound came from his lips. Sound unlike anything she'd heard before.

She stared at him for a long moment. "En-ee-kee -"

He chuckled. "Enkoodabaoo."

The word was long and strange, but she wanted desperately to show him the respect of using his true name. Thus far, he'd been the kindest and most patient man she'd ever met. "Any-key-dee... Any-key? I'm sorry," she said, blushing.

He shook his head and smiled.

"Does it mean something?"

He hopped up and marched across their small camp, pulling a canteen from the horse's saddlebag. He handed it to her. "It means, One Who Walks Alone."

She took the canteen and frowned. What a sad name, she thought. "Any-key... Any... How did you say it again?"

"You may call me Joseph. That is the name they gave me in the Christian School."

Her brow furrowed and she shook her head. "But that's not your name."

He stopped and stared at her a moment. "No. No, it is not. Still, I've yet to meet a white man who could properly call me by my true name."

Her face flushed. "Any-key-dee-ai-"

His brows shot up. "Yes, very close. Enkoodabaoo." He took his time, squatting down across from her to watch her face.

She felt small in his gaze but did her best to repeat him. "Any-key-day-boo?"

"Perfect. We'll have time to practice," he said, beaming.

His smile disarmed her instantly. She shook her head as though she might loose these affectionate thoughts from her mind.

Don't think of him like that, Cadence. Remember how the last fella you fancied turned out.

Shannon Bell's equally disarming smile flooded to mind.

"Will you help me learn it? I'm sorry I'm having such trouble."

Joseph came around the fire to sit beside her, patting his hand on hers. "Believe me, you couldn't offend me if you tried, Cadence. You're the first person to ask my true name in a very – very long time."

The tone of his voice hurt her heart. That tone betrayed the source of his name –One Who Walks Alone.

"How old were you when they made you – made you Joseph?"

Joseph gave an appraising look. "I'd seen twelve winters when they took me from my family."

Cadence's chest tightened. "They took you?"

He gave her a half smile. "They did. They took me, my cousins – all the children and put us in Christian schools. It was meant to teach us the white man's culture, learn his language. I remember the day they cut my hair, I cried for a week straight."

Cadence leaned toward Joseph then, and without even knowing what she was doing, kissed him.

Joseph stiffened, but after a moment, his lips softened. He reached up to touch her face and kissed her back.

Cadence felt breathless for an instant. She hadn't planned to kiss Joseph, but at that moment, hearing him describe what happened to him as a boy, after seeing those young boys at the agency school with their short hair and shy demeanors – it caused such a surge of affection for him that she would've wrapped herself around him if she could.

His fingertips were soft against her cheek, and he moved them back into her mass of light hair. The touch of his fingertips only further inspired shivers. The gesture reminded her of Shannon, but she pushed the thought aside.

Joseph was her savior, her protector. His kiss didn't carry the tension of danger like Shannon's had. It felt safe. It felt like something she wanted to feel again, but after a long moment, Joseph pulled from her, gazing into her eyes with a surprised, but pleased expression on his tan face.

"That was a nice surprise, petal."

Her chest tightened instantly.

Shannon wasn't the first man to call her petal, but he'd been the last. The memory made her stomach drop even as her cheeks grew hot. Cadence turned her eyes away from him, pulling her hair down over her cheek to hide her face. He watched her a moment, then reached up and pushed the hair behind her ear.

"You might be the most surprising woman I've ever met, Cadence."

She exhaled. Despite how his innocent word affected her, it was these words that worked far stronger magic. She offered him a smile.

A moment later, Joseph moved closer to the fire, returning his attention to cooking the rabbit for their dinner.

They sat in an energized silence for a long time before Cadence finally spoke.

"I promise I'll learn how to say your name."

Joseph glanced over his shoulder. "I promise I'll smile every time you say it."

CHAPTER SIX

THEY REMAINED ON THE trail for days. Joseph made a point to travel along the river, making sure if Cadence needed to take a moment, she could wash without having to explain herself. She'd never been more grateful to a man in her life.

By the fourth day, her courses were passed. Still, she missed the comfort of a bed more than she could express. She made a point not to share this with Joseph, but that didn't stop her from groaning or grumbling as she dropped off the horse or rose from her bed each morning. She was sure he was laughing at her for it.

An Algonquin who'd spent much of his life sleeping under the stars having to tend to a soft footed white woman.

What an odd pair they must make.

She hadn't found the courage yet to kiss Joseph again, though she'd wanted to. And she was beginning to think the desire was mutual. She'd caught him watching her more than once – as she stood in the river in little more than her petticoats, washing out her linens, or when she'd curled into the fur hides and closed her eyes. Joseph remained a gentleman in all ways, hunting for her meals, offering the warmest hide each night before bed, tending to the fire to be sure she was warm. He treated her better than any person she'd ever known. Cadence was beginning to feel guilty that she couldn't offer him anything in return – save for danger.

They reached the Palmer Outpost by the fifth day, and Joseph hopped off the horse to lead Thunder into the small community with Cadence on her back.

"Hopefully, they'll think I'm your servant and not your captor," he'd said, chuckling as he clucked to the horse to move along.

Yet this didn't make Cadence smile. There was nothing funny to her about people believing Joseph was either a slave or a criminal instead of the great man he was. Still, Cadence did as he asked, riding along on the horse with her head held high.

Putting on airs wasn't something she enjoyed, but she knew damn well how to look proud. She'd done it every time she went into the streets of Cheyenne to run errands alone.

The higher you hold your head, the harder it is to hear the jeers of those beneath you.

That was what her mother always said.

Cadence glanced down at the people who milled around the buildings of the Palmer Outpost. There were several buildings for the small post – a barn, a trading post, a post office, as well as a few houses and outbuildings of the families that called Palmer Outpost home. She noted rather swiftly that they were all men.

Cadence glanced into a small tavern and saw the only other women she'd seen since the Indian Agency and smirked.

Spoke too soon, she thought.

"Alright, I'll go inside and see if I can't get a room for the night, yes?"

Cadence fought not to openly sigh on the back of Joseph's horse, but she nodded her assent. He disappeared inside a moment later, leaving her to sit atop Thunder and feel the eyes of half a dozen men on her. They either openly stared at her or gave her one too many glances as they made their way by. She fought to keep her regal exterior, ignoring their curious glares.

A long moment passed before she heard raised voices coming from inside the tavern. Cadence listened intently as the surrounding men also moved closer to the tavern to see what the fuss was about. She heard an unfamiliar voice in the office, hollering his distaste.

"You ain't got no business here. I don't care who you're traveling with, I don't rent to no reds!"

Cadence felt her blood boil, instantly. She kicked her leg up and over the horse, dropping to the ground with a loud clamor. She tied Thunder's reins just outside the office, pushing past the men who stood there leering through the door or the windows to catch a glimpse of the drama within. Cadence shoved the door open and stormed inside, slamming the door in the faces of the curious men.

She entered the office to find Joseph standing on one side of a long counter, his hands in the air in a gesture of placation as the bearded man on the other side spit venom across the counter.

"You got some nerve comin in here thinkin you've some kinda right. What business is it of yours who's been through these parts? I ain't your fuckin secretary."

"Enough!" Cadence hollered, marching up to the counter to meet the growling figure. He wore a white button down shirt and black suspenders – the common garb of a clerk, or any other manner of respectable person, but there was nothing respectable about the rest of him. His teeth were so crooked, Cadence was sure they'd been punched askew one too many times in a bar room brawl, and his breath was as foul as his mood. He had white guck collected in the corners of his mouth, and his mustache had grown well past his upper lip. She stared at the man with the mind of a tavern proprietor and thought instantly that this man would have been turned out on his ear before she'd have served him. What right did such a vagabond have berating a gentleman like Joseph?

Simply because he was native.

"I'll have you apologize to my friend," she said, pointing a finger at the man's face like a stern nanny.

"I'll do no such thi -"

"You *will*!"

"I apologize." The man clapped his hands onto the counter as though trying to kill a fly, and his expression changed. Cadence stopped dead, making sure to consider every word she said. He'd done as she commanded, instantly, and it clearly terrified him.

Cadence could feel it – feel the strange connection she had to this man, to whatever will he had. She could bend it and shape it as she pleased now but knowing that gave her pause. Joseph was her only friend, her fondest companion. What would he think if he saw her bending the will of this man like gold in her teeth?

Cadence swallowed. "You will rent us a room, please. We will be out of your hair early in the morning. And you will give my companion no further trouble, do you understand me?"

The clerk turned from the counter and pulled a key from a hook on the wall. He slammed it down on the counter, glaring at her with a nervous glint in his eye. He was fighting to keep his dower mood, but behind that angry gaze, she saw the very same look she'd seen in Miss George's eyes – trepidation. He could be angry all he liked. He still didn't dare cross her. He couldn't.

Cadence glanced down at the key on the counter. The tag read #3.

"That'll do nicely. Thank you. Do you need anything further, Joseph?"

Joseph's eyebrows shot up and he glanced between the angry clerk and Cadence once, then twice before finally shaking his head. "No, no. I'm quite content. Thank you, sir."

Cadence snatched the key up from the counter and turned for the door with Joseph following just behind her. She glanced back at him as she untied Thunder's reins from her post.

He was fighting back a smile.

They settled Thunder into one of the barn stalls with some grain and hay, then Joseph hauled the saddlebags over his shoulder, and they headed for the stairs. The tavern kept a second, outdoor staircase, wooden and somewhat rickety, leading up to the second floor and the rooms within. Cadence marched up the steps, glaring down at anyone who might be watching her.

The clerk had lit a fire in her. She felt powerful and fearless. She'd been able to shut a man down. A grown man – put him in his place whether he wanted to be put there or not.

Despite the nightmares she still suffered since that night in the Red Onion, she was beginning to see Shannon's actions as a gift. Whatever he'd done to her, whatever he'd turned her into – perhaps she could use it for some good.

Oh god, she thought. What if she could use it on Malcolm Green?

She shook her head as though someone else spoke and pressed her hands to the front of her dress, willing herself calm.

Don't become power hungry like Joseph said. It feels nice to be taken seriously. It feels nice to have your word respected, but she couldn't let that change who she was. She wasn't a tyrant. She refused to become one.

But my god did it feel good making that bastard eat crow, she thought.

The sound of Joseph dumping the saddlebags onto the floor startled her around. She found him standing by the door of the small bedroom, his clothes and hair still dusty from days of riding. She watched him a moment, waiting to understand the strange energy in the room. He stared at the floorboards as though he might burn a hole through them with his eyes.

Cadence took a step toward him. "Joseph? Are you alright? That bastard didn't upset you, did -"

Joseph looked up at her and his eyes stilled her words. He looked at her with a strangeness now – an intensity she'd never seen in another person's eyes before.

She swallowed. "Joseph?"

He moved across the room with such lithe speed that Cadence feared her eyes were playing tricks. An instant later, Joseph's arms were around her middle, pulling her into him. She went limp in his arms, letting him pull her against him. He stared down at her with such an intense fire in his eyes, she feared he might hurt her. She'd been close to him many times – on the horse or in the river, but as he held her in his arms, only now did she realize just how tall he was.

Joseph didn't speak, but instead stared down at her, letting his fingers graze up her cheek and into her hair again. She shivered at the touch but couldn't speak.

Joseph's eyes moved over her face, settling on her lips. "You kissed me once."

Cadence opened her mouth, but no words came.

"I'd like to return the favor," he said, letting his thumb graze over her lower lip. She could feel his breath on her face, warm and clean, unlike any man who'd come this close to her before, steaming from a night of drinking bourbon or worse. She clutched her hand in the fabric of his shirt, feeling small and precious in his arms.

She steadied herself and met his gaze. "Then what are you waiting for?"

Joseph's expression changed, baring his teeth like some beast as he bent down and hauled her up into his arms. Cadence threw her arms around his neck to hold on as Joseph carried her across the room and pressed her into the wall. She was pinned there, his body moving between her legs as his lips found hers. He bit her lower lip, drawing a startled shriek from her, but when he released her, she met his eyes with a new fervor. This was how she'd always imagined a man would take her – with fervor, with passion. All memory of Stephen Goldrup vanished as she grabbed Joseph's hair and bit his lip right back. Yet unlike Joseph, she bit hard.

He winced, pulling away just enough to touch one of his dusty fingers to his lip. He was bleeding.

Cadence felt her heart shoot into her throat. She hadn't meant to bite him so hard, she hadn't meant to hurt. Yet in the instant it took to make him bleed, she'd never felt so aroused in her life.

Joseph held his hand aloft, showing her the blood, and smiled. "You're going to pay for that."

"Oh god," she muttered as Joseph pulled her from the wall, turned her around and threw up her skirts. She squealed, flailing her hands back, half laughing and half crying out as Joseph dropped down on the edge of the bed and yanked her down across his lap. An instant later, Joseph smacked her ass. Cadence gasped, then wailed in response. The wail descended instantly to laughter.

Joseph met her gaze, his eyebrows shooting up. "Laughter? Oh, I think you need another one."

He wound up, ready to smack her again, but Cadence scrambled from his lap, covering her backside with her hands. She rolled onto her back on the hardwood floor, her hands out to hold Joseph at bay. This version of him startled and enchanted her. To know the kindness and gentle way he showed her in every other moment, only to see this version appear in private – she'd been unprepared for how fond of him it made her. She wanted him now more than she'd ever wanted anything in her life.

He smiled down at her. "Do you want me to take you?"

Cadence's eyes went wide, and she searched for words. Had there been a more affirmative word than, 'yes,' she'd have screamed it.

Joseph smiled. "I'll take your silence as a maybe."

"Yes, I want you," she said, her words coming in barely a whisper.

He heard her. Without another word, Joseph pulled down his suspenders and dropped to his knees before her. She watched him with rapt attention as he unbuttoned the blue shirt he wore, baring his dark chest to her. He was the color of late autumn and as he lowered himself down onto her, he smelled like autumn, too. It was hypnotic.

Cadence gasped as Joseph pressed himself between her legs. The pressure of his weight moving against her in a deliberate way. His lips found hers before she could make a sound, and the taste of his blood still lingered there.

A part of her moved with caution. It was as though she feared giving herself over to the desire would make him stop. Stephen had always wanted a timid girl, a submissive girl. He'd told her that was what all men wanted in their women.

Then why had Joseph smiled so wickedly when she bit him? Why had he hardened against her when she let go?

Joseph's tongue pierced her lips and she inhaled him, shocked by the sensation. This felt like nothing she'd experienced before, and she almost feared him seeing it.

He released her, letting her breathe as he rose to his knees again and began pulling the buttons of his trousers open. Cadence held her breath, watching as every new inch of Joseph's skin came into view, looking so foreign, and yet so perfect. He stopped, letting his pants hang open without betraying view of what lay beneath. She groaned in disappointment before catching herself.

Joseph's eyes went wide, and he beamed. "Oh, you are a ferocious thing, aren't you?"

Cadence felt her heart race. She wanted to say yes. She wanted to scream yes and then tear into him, but before she could, Joseph's hands were at the ties of her dress, yanking every knot free. She grabbed the hem of her bodice and pulled it open to him as they both moved with fury to undress her. The dress fell about her waist and Joseph grabbed the collar of her chemise, yanking the hem down to bare her breasts. She heard the tell-tale sound of the fabric ripping, but she didn't care. She could barely think as Joseph pinned her back down to the floor and planted his mouth over her breast, biting her there with just enough ferocity to draw a yelp. Then his touch softened, and he began to knead her flesh with his tongue. Cadence's head fell back as she succumbed to the sensation, moaning in relief and desire. The sensation drove her, causing heat to build between her legs. She curled her hands into his black hair, feeling the braid loosen as she did.

He moved up the length of her then, devouring her mouth as his hands made quick work of tugging her petticoats off. She felt the cool of the air against her thighs and her breath caught in her throat. The notion that Joseph would be having his way with her summoned a strange excitement and almost fear. She'd only ever been touched by two men before now, and though she'd wanted Shannon very much when she let him touch her, she hadn't known Shannon the way she knew Joseph. She hadn't spent days in his company, learning his walk, his smell, the way he treated everyone, from the man in the office to his horse. She knew Joseph, and she wanted all of him. Not just his body – all of him.

He rose to his knees, hooked his thumbs under the waistband of his trousers and met her gaze. He clearly knew she wanted to see him, and he smiled.

Joseph lowered his trousers and his erection sprung from beneath. She gasped softly at the sight of him, and he only grinned wider to hear it. Without a word, he lowered himself over her again, pressing his lips to hers as he let the hard shape of him move against her. Cadence braced for him, but he didn't enter her then. Instead, he kissed her deeply, moving against her, deliberately holding back. Cadence dragged her nails down his bare back, grabbing hold of his smooth backside to urge him onward.

He chuckled softly into her mouth. "Tsk, tsk. I'm still punishing you for that bite," he said, grinning against her lips.

She opened her mouth and clamped her teeth down onto his jaw, letting him feel her, but not wanting to hurt.

He groaned. "You are a rare woman, Cadence."

He loomed over her now, his hair falling loose. Cadence looked up into his familiar face, relishing in this new mischief that arousal played there.

"You are a rare man," she said, and she was sure she'd never meant anything more.

He stared at her a long moment, still pressing himself between her legs in rhythm, slipping against the wetness he found there.

Finally, Cadence felt him move with purpose and she braced herself. Joseph stared down at her as he pushed into her, his eyes fluttering with pleasure as her body welcomed him with ease. Cadence gasped, feeling a tinge of almost pain that instantly gave way to relief. She'd been sore with need before he entered her, now she felt complete.

Cadence moved her hands over his back, hooking under his arms to gain purchase. Joseph moved deliberately, taking his time, watching her for a response. She couldn't help but whimper as he moved. He felt unlike anything she'd felt before. He moved with confidence, making a point to smile each time she cried out, only to turn his attention to repeating the cause over and over until she was breathless and unable to cry at all.

His movements gained purpose, driving deeper and harder into her as her shoulders rocked over the hardwood floor. She clutched his backside, pulling him deeper with each thrust, letting her head fall back as his movements did their work. Her body was shaking beneath him, tense and taut and waiting for release. Joseph drove into her, soft hums and groans escaping his lips every few seconds, letting her know she wasn't the only one coming undone.

Cadence found herself watching his body, curling into herself to see the place where his dark skin met her paleness. The dark hair around his sex pressing into her, feeling him move inside her. It was all becoming too much, too fast. She gasped, watching him thrust into her, then gasped again as her body tensed around him. He groaned in appreciation as her body convulsed, her legs jerking behind his back.

Cadence yelped in response to the strange sensation – then wailed as it doubled in force and rushed through her body in waves. It was all she could do not to scream for mercy as Joseph continued his thrusts, groaning in approval as she curled into him, shaking.

The sensation peaked and subsided, leaving her trembling beneath him. She looked up into his beautiful face, watching the waves of black hair sway as he thrust faster now, his groans rising to one constant growl.

Finally, he rose to his knees, took hold of her thighs, and pulled her into him, drawing a whole new round of cries as he thrust deeply. She watched him in rapt attention, wanting to see him enjoy her. Joseph thrust one last time, and the growl stopped. He moved in her once – twice more, then exhaled, loosening his hold on her thighs.

Cadence felt the place where they joined throbbing as he slowly pulled away. He slumped down to lie beside her on the floor. His body was bare, glistening with sweat, the dust of their days of riding pooling at his collar bone.

He gave a satisfied groan. "Mm, I'd been waiting to do that until I could offer you a bed. I see that wasn't necessary, now."

Cadence laughed, glancing over at the brass bedframe. She ran her finger over his damp skin, wanting to paint herself on him. Though she didn't speak the thoughts, she silently hoped they might christen the bed as well before the night was over.

Joseph brushed his hair out of his face and smiled at her, glancing to the dust on his skin. "Perhaps we should pay for a bath?"

Cadence rolled onto her side, planting a kiss on his injured lips. He grabbed her hair, pulling her against him until his teeth grazed hers – he was grinning ear to ear.

CHAPTER SEVEN

CADENCE HADN'T WOKEN TO the sound of a rooster since she was young. The city of Cheyenne had expanded over the years and much of the farmland was pushed back for further enterprise. She hadn't thought to miss it when she woke to the early risers of Cheyenne's busy streets, but now – as she lay in a tired old cot under a cracked window, she almost forgot how troubled her life had become. The dingy white curtains flitted in the breeze from outside, swaying over her as light began to fill the small room. Joseph made love to her that morning before leaving to find them something to eat. She'd thought to protest, worried he might cross paths with the surly clerk again, but then she remembered.

That clerk wouldn't be giving him any trouble again soon.

They'd both washed the night before, making love again in the copper bath tub down the hall from their room. She was sure their behavior was brazen. A white woman sleeping in a room with a native man was enough to cause an angry mob, but Joseph refused to worry, slipping out to collect their breakfast. Cadence stretched in her bed, the smoky old nightgown twisted around her waist from where she'd hoisted it to give Joseph access to her. She'd wanted to argue with Joseph for spending his own money on her comfort, but he wouldn't be swayed. Cadence wondered how Calvin would feel to hear the greatest gentleman she'd ever met wasn't even a shade of white.

She cringed in the bed and pushed the thought of Calvin aside just as the rooster called again. She took a deep breath. Who knew where the day would take them, but at least she'd known a little comfort?

There came a gentle knock at the door before it opened, and Joseph appeared there, grinning at her.

She sighed. He crossed the room, settling on the edge of the bed. Despite his bath the night before, he still smelled of horses and dust and smoke. She was growing fond of the smell with each passing moment she spent with him.

"Here we are. We have some kind of -"

Cadence snatched the bundle of brown paper from his hand and opened it to find three hard boiled eggs, cold cooked bacon, two apples, and a big slab of cornbread crumbling in the middle of it. She tore a massive chunk from the cornbread and smashed it into her mouth, letting the crumbs fall down the front of her nightshirt.

For the first time in well over a week, she was hungry for something other than Joseph's magical smoked jerky.

"Are you rested? I hope you slept well?"

She smiled at his sarcastic grin. He knew full well how little she'd slept. He laughed, helping her wipe the crumbs away as he climbed into the bed beside her.

"I had a wonderful night. Thank you!" She said, her mouth half full.

Joseph smiled, snatching a hardboiled egg from the bundle. "I'm glad. We should probably be moving along soon enough."

Cadence nodded, sighing as she tasted a slab of bacon. Cadence offered Joseph a piece of cornbread before devouring the last of it. She shot him a sideways glance as he calmly ate his breakfast. His hair was braided today, leaving a long train of glistening black hanging down his right shoulder.

"I was surprised to find the ladies working this early," he said, dipping the egg into a smear of bacon grease.

"Oh, were you? You clearly haven't spent a lot of time with prostitutes, I take it?"

Joseph chuckled. "Don't hold it against me."

She laughed, brushing aside the cornbread crumbs from the edge of the bed despite fully intending to add more.

"Now, that isn't entirely fair. You haven't spent too much time with them either if I recall."

"How do you figure?" Cadence asked, her mouth only half full.

Joseph popped the last bite of egg in his mouth and pressed his nose to her hair, inhaling her before slumping back onto the pillow. "Well, if I recall the Red Onion didn't allow such things, no?"

She shrugged. "No, not since my daddy put a stop to it. When I was little, I spent quite a bit of time around such ladies."

Joseph propped his head up on his hand. "Really? That's a surprise. What changed? Did your father find the 'Lord?'?"

He said the word 'Lord' with a tinge of sarcasm. Cadence imagined how Joseph must have taken the bible stories when he was taken from his family and put in a 'Christian' school. The more she thought about it, the less Cadence could find Christian about any of it.

Cadence stopped chewing for a moment, remembering the year her father turned all the girls out from the upstairs of the Red Onion.

He'd been good to them, women who worked when they pleased for as much as they pleased. They always had a safe place, and a stern boss to keep the rabble from getting too rough or handsy. Still, he'd completely changed his business when Cadence was nine years old.

She swallowed a big bite of cornbread and stared at the crumbs on the paper. "Well, we had a girl working in the Onion named Abigail. She was real nice to me, taught me how to write my cursive letters and how to make change from two bits. The last year Pa let girls work upstairs, Abigail had started takin this fella from out of town. Some prospector or a miner, I don't know which. Anyway, she fell in love with him."

Joseph ran his fingers through her hair, listening intently as he played with a long strand of blonde curls.

"She thought he was gonna take her away from it all. Marry her, but when she told him how she felt, he laughed in her face. She was all sort of upset."

"I can imagine," Joseph said softly. "What happened?"

Cadence shrugged, popping the last bite of cornbread in her mouth. "She hanged herself."

Joseph's fingers stilled for a long moment before he returned to his idle playing with her hair.

"There used to be a beam in the hallway outside my bedroom. After she hanged herself, I woke up to the sound of something gently banging at my door. I got out of bed and tried to see who was there, but my door wouldn't open. There was something against it."

Joseph's arm moved across her stomach, pulling her closer to him.

"I panicked and started screaming for my Pa. I was afraid I'd be trapped forever. Next thing I knew, I heard his voice out in the hallway telling me everything was alright, that I needed to climb back in bed and go back to sleep. That he loved me."

Cadence frowned, letting the memory of her father settle into her mind wholly. She'd rarely contemplated her father since her mother died. Now, remembering how much he'd loved her was causing a tinge of new pain at the thought of losing the Red Onion. Still, she fought to ignore the lump gathering in her throat.

"I did as I was told. When I got up later on, there was no sign of what had happened. They told me Abigail had moved away when I noticed she wasn't around. A week later, Pa sent all the girls away, told em to find a new place to take their customers. They didn't like it, but they all respected him for it. Said he'd die before he'd run the risk of his little girl seeing something like that again."

"He sounds like he deserved that respect."

Cadence pressed a knuckle to the corner of her eye, wiping away the tears that were gathering there. "He did. It wasn't until I was a grown woman that my Ma told me the real reason why Pa stopped renting the rooms out to girls. It's why I still won't to this day."

Cadence groaned as Joseph's hold on her tightened. He didn't open his mouth, but his arms spoke volumes as he held her tight against him. Finally, Cadence did her best to break the mood, snatching up another slab of bacon. "You better dig in before I eat all of this," she said, forcing a smile.

When they were done eating, Cadence stood up, brushing the crumbs from her nightshirt just as Joseph rolled to the edge of the bed. "I'll let you get dressed, while I get Thunder saddled up. If you'd meet me at the West corner, we can head out."

She nodded and watched Joseph climb out of the bed with a groan. He crossed the room to her, putting his hand to the curve of her lower back and pulling her to him. He kissed then, and the kiss was different – timeless somehow, like the kiss a man gives to his wife of fifty years. Cadence met his eyes and they stood in silence for a long moment, then he slipped out the bedroom door.

She went to the foot of the cot to check her dress. The long skirts crinkled under her fingers, but the fabric was dry and smelled of smoke. The tiny woodstove in the corner had done its job. She was dressed and folding up the nightshirt a moment later.

The outpost was a quiet little oasis hidden in the plains, the Palmer family farmhouse just a hundred yards outside the post. It was quieter now in the early morning, the air crackling with a cold mist.

Cadence sauntered through the downstairs of the outpost, nodding to the surly clerk behind the counter as she went.

He gave her a strange nod.

Outside was cooler than the day before, the winds kicking up with purpose. The distant clang of glass wind chimes was tinkling away in the winds, coupled by annoyed horses and bulls who were simply trying to graze on the grass. Cadence turned toward the west corner but didn't get a chance to move as a figure sauntered past her from the post office, his gait betraying purpose. She turned, letting her eyes follow him as she waited for him to notice her.

Shannon Bell sauntered past as though oblivious to her presence. She froze, waiting, hoping her eyes would focus and the vision would be a lie. It wasn't. She held perfectly still, as though doing so might blend her into her surroundings.

He glanced back her way, then stopped.

"I know you," he said, smirking.

She swallowed.

Shannon took a step toward her, and she recoiled. Something about his eyes, the way he looked at her felt strange now – dangerous. She stepped back again, Shannon closing in until her shoulder was pressed against the wall of the trading post.

"What can I do for you, girlie?" He asked, putting a hand on the wall over her shoulder, cornering her there. He shot her another smile and turned his eyes to the wall at her shoulder. "Not the best likeness, I'd say, but it certainly gets the point across?"

Shannon took a piece of her hair between his fingers and twirled it.

Something felt wrong. He didn't feel the way he usually did. Shannon Bell could command a space like a king. Now he felt no different than one of the smarmy drunks that leered at her on rowdy nights at the saloon – foreboding, dark, threatening. Now he felt cold – unsafe. Cadence turned her face away from him just as a ruckus erupted in the nearby post office.

Shannon grinned, giving her chin a pinch before he turned back toward the barn and disappeared inside. The post office shook with the sounds of screaming, and a tall, gray bearded man came bursting out of the trading post, a shotgun in his hands. He barreled right past her, heading toward the sounds of a woman screaming. Cadence turned to follow, coming around the corner just in time to see a woman led out of the post office, her hands pressed to her stomach as though she might be sick. Her hands were covered in blood.

Cadence gasped at the sight, feeling anguish at the familiarity of the woman's plight. She stepped away, wanting to help, to be of some use to anyone, but a pair of hands grabbed her by the shoulders and yanked her under the stairs along the trading post wall.

She froze, watching three men come pouring out of the barn and general store, hollering for the woman. Cadence almost didn't want to turn around, half afraid it was Shannon holding her there. Despite the last time she'd seen him and let her guard down, this time didn't feel the same. This time, Shannon frightened her.

The hands at her shoulders spun her around and she found Joseph just behind her, his finger pressed to his lips to signal silence. She tucked in under the stairs and listened.

"Jesus, don't go in there! Somebody ride for the Sheriff! It's a god damn mess inside!"

Cadence gasped, feeling her stomach grow tight. "What happened?" She asked. She didn't need to be told, her heart already knew.

"Who's in there? Who's in there, dammit?" One of the men was hollering as he came running.

Cadence heard the commotion around her, turning away from the sight of the woman as the chaos unfolded.

"Two of the fellas from Cheyenne are in pieces in there. Poor Mrs. Palmer found the bastards."

"Send for the doctor, then!"

"Naw. Fellas ain't gonna be needin a doctor."

Cadence felt cornered there again, but this time, it wasn't Shannon keeping her trapped, it was his deeds. He'd done it again. He'd professed his innocence by the river, and she'd let herself believe him. Yet, here she was –

She stopped cold, unable to even form a thought as she turned toward the wall of the trading post.

She replayed Shannon's words as she stared at the piece of paper nailed to the sideboard. "Not the best likeness," he'd said. "But it gets the point across."

Joseph noticed her expression and turned toward the wall as well.

REWARD $500

Reward for the ARREST and DETENTION of Cadence Delacouer

Cadence stared at the poster as her mouth went dry. The picture wasn't exact by any means, but it was enough. It went on to describe her in detail – 5'7", blonde hair, blue eyes.

"We have to go," Joseph whispered, pulling her toward the barn.

The notion of going toward the barn broke her from her spell. She jerked her arm away, almost frantic. "No! He's in there."

Joseph's eyes went wide. "Who is?"

"Shannon Bell!"

He grabbed her, pulling her toward the barn doors as he tugged his knife from his belt. Joseph rushed inside, pulling her behind him, the long hunting knife in his right hand. The voices outside began to rise, drawing nervous whinnies from the few horses stabled in the barn. Cadence spotted Joseph's horse in the far stall, her brown face over the door, shaking her head up and down as though propelling her master onward. Cadence tried to pull from Joseph's grasp, but he wouldn't let go.

He turned back to her. "Where did he go?"

"I don't know," she hissed. "He went inside. I didn't follow him in!"

"Why didn't you call for me?"

She stopped, trying to pull away.

"Cadence! Why didn't you call?"

She couldn't answer. Why hadn't she called for Joseph – for anyone? Why had she stayed quiet when he cornered her against the wall? Why hadn't she told Joseph he was at the river, and above all, the night Calvin died, when Shannon forced her to eat her stepfather's heart, why hadn't she screamed for help until he was gone?

"I don't know," she said, hardly able to form the words.

Joseph released his hold on her and barreled across the barn, releasing his horse from her stall. He tossed a bridle over her ears and led her back toward the doors of the barn, glancing into each stall as he went.

"Why the hell you two been followin me?"

Joseph met Cadence's eyes and they both froze for an instant. Joseph moved forward, a scowl on his face as he fast approached, hunting knife displayed in his hand. Then he stopped, holding his hands up as Shannon Bell appeared at Cadence's shoulder.

"We don't want any trouble," Joseph started, but Cadence gasped as an arm moved across her collar, grabbing her around the shoulders. Shannon yanked her back against him, holding her firmly as he brandished a pistol in his other hand. "You got three seconds to tell me why you're followin me, so I suggest you start talkin."

Joseph splayed his fingers, letting the hunting knife fall from his hand. "You don't need to hurt her, friend. She means you no harm."

"Friend?" He said, repeating it with a lilt to his voice. He turned his face into her cheek and inhaled. Her whole body tensed. He felt so wrong.

"I'd say we're more than friends, ain't we girlie?"

She stifled a cry. The comment made her feel ashamed.

"She's not screaming now, I'm sure she won't scream once you're gone if you just let her go -"

"Shut up and explain! Why are you hunting me? Cause I know I ain't the only one of my kind here, ladies and gents!"

She froze. Dear god, Joseph would know now. "Because I'm wanted for your crimes, damn it!" Cadence said, letting her voice rise as he tightened his grip around her.

"Is that so? What, you hopin to bring me in, then? Give me up to the Marshals? Collect my bounty? There ain't no bounty on me, honey. Just on you. Maybe I'll do some collectin myself, hmm?"

Outside the voices were rising again as people rushed from building to building. "I'll ride for the Sheriff. You get Mrs. Palmer back up to the house. Get her settled!"

Shannon tightened his hold and pulled her backward toward the barn doors. Then, he glanced out in either direction, pointed the pistol at Joseph, and turned to press his lips to Cadence's ear. He kissed her and let go, disappearing out the door. Joseph lunged toward her, taking hold of her before she fell to the ground in relief and shock.

"You're alright?" He asked, barely waiting for a nod before he dove out the barn doors in pursuit. Cadence sat there a long moment, staring at the dirt of the barn floor, wisps of grain and old hay skittering across it in drafts from outside. Only a moment passed before Joseph reappeared, snatching up the bridle of his horse and hauling Cadence to her feet. He led both Cadence and the horse out into the open. Cadence watched him climb on, then stared at the hand he held out to her.

"Cadence. We have to go!"

She shook her head, glancing back at the poster on the wall. "They're gonna think I did this. Again."

There was no inflection in her voice. She felt so defeated at that moment, she almost wanted Joseph to turn her in. At least there'd be something in it for him. Otherwise, she'd just be more trouble for this kind man, and she detested the idea of dragging him down with her.

"Come on, we haven't got time!" Joseph said, his tone dropping to a gravelly and stern place. She took a breath, hearing the commotion inside the trading post. She stood frozen for just a moment longer, then lunged back toward the trading post, and snatched the Wanted poster from the wall. Cadence hurried back to Joseph and let him haul her up onto the horse before taking off from the far corner of the barn.

CHAPTER EIGHT

CADENCE LET THE CRUMPLED paper grow damp in her sweaty hands. She sat on the back of Joseph's horse willing the picture on the poster to disappear. Yet each time she looked, it was still there, and each time she looked, the picture looked more and more like her.

"It will all be well once we find him – again," Joseph said, and his tone betrayed suspicion. Cadence hurt to hear it after the kindnesses he'd shown her for the past few days. He'd put himself in danger to protect her, all in the name of finding the man truly responsible for her supposed crimes. Yet each time they'd crossed paths with the murderer, she'd protected him through inaction. She'd never mentioned a word of his presence to her protector.

She didn't blame his suspicion. She felt haunted by it herself.

"Did he compel you?" Joseph asked as they rode over the plains on the blustery afternoon. "Is that why you didn't tell me?"

He spoke of the encounter by the river when Shannon held her underwater to shield her from the Cheyenne posse – with their Wanted posters and guns. This was the one that troubled them both most. Why didn't she tell Joseph when he returned?

"I fell in," she'd said. Not, "Shannon Bell half drowned me, but he said he had a good reason."

"You must tell me when you see him, Cadence."

"I know," she said, mumbling half to herself.

They traveled for a full day before a familiar cluster of trees startled her to attention. She straightened in the saddle, holding onto Joseph as tightly as she could. "Wait, that isn't the same -?"

"It is," Joseph said. Then he dismounted the horse, leading her the rest of the way by the reins.

Cadence swallowed hard. They were heading back East. People might recognize her the closer they travelled to Cheyenne. Was Joseph planning to turn her in? There was a reward, after all.

"Why are we back here?"

Joseph dropped down to his knees and played with the dirt a moment, rolling it around in his fingers. "Following his trail. This is where he headed."

"Back to our camp?"

"It seems so," Joseph said, turning to offer a hand to her. She felt uneasy to be drawing closer to Cheyenne as opposed to further away. Unlike the Palmer Outpost, the people of Cheyenne would know her by name, even if the portrait on her wanted poster wasn't quite accurate.

Joseph offered her one of the stained fur hides before he turned his attention to the fire. He wasn't speaking to her as he normally would. He hadn't had much to say since their encounter with Shannon in the barn. Cadence feared he was angry with her enough to have turned his kindness. She couldn't say she didn't deserve it.

Still, the memory of his fingers playing with her hair hurt her heart. What if she'd turned his affections? What if Joseph never wanted to touch her again?

The fire was roaring in a matter of moments, and soon Joseph was gone into the trees, marching down to the creek to find them something for supper.

Cadence sat in silence watching the tiny sparks rising from the fire, drifting into the dark and disappearing long before they hit the tree branches overhead. Cadence tugged the fur hide close to her ears, fighting to keep the cold out. It was nearly impossible – it wasn't just the night air that left her cold.

"What did he mean?"

Joseph's voice startled her from her thoughts. "What?" She said.

"Shannon. What he said. More than friends -"

"It don't mean nothing," she said, her voice going shrill.

"- And that he wasn't the only one of his kind."

Cadence stared at him, her mouth hanging open as she searched for words. Shannon had betrayed her in that moment. Whether his apparent disregard was a show or not, he'd told her secret. Had Joseph not known damn well what Shannon was, she might have gotten through this day without having to confess herself. Joseph stared at her from across the camp, their dinner hanging limp in his left hand, his hunting knife in the right. She half feared he'd turn the blade on her the second he knew what she was.

It wouldn't be the first time a lover turned on her.

"Cadence. You tell me what he meant," he said and pointed the knife in her direction.

Instead of speaking, Cadence's face contorted not in fear, but in grief. The anger that played on Joseph's dark face hurt far worse than she'd been prepared. Shannon Bell, the man she'd unwittingly protected from capture more than once had managed to lose her the only solace she had left in the world.

Shannon took everything from her, and he was still doing it now, without shedding a drop of blood.

Tears welled over and rolled down her cheeks as Joseph waited for her to speak. When no words came, he tossed the rabbit down beside her and marched toward his horse.

"No, please don't go!" She cried, jumping up to follow him.

He shook his head, packing up his satchel as he grumbled to himself in another language. "You haven't been honest with me since the first moment. Not once. I've half a mind to think you were in on the whole thing. Foolish of me."

"No! I would never hurt anyone!"

"So you say."

He didn't look over his shoulder as he packed his knife into his belt and turned for the hollowed tree. He pulled the saddle from atop it and turned back toward the horse.

"Please, Any-key-day-aib..."

She lost the word, but he stopped a moment, the saddle still in his hands.

"I promise I'll be honest. I will. I won't give you reason to suspect me again. I swear, please!"

He turned on her. "Then tell me the truth now! Why did he say he wasn't the only one of his kind?"

Cadence growled in frustration and grief, but the words followed, nonetheless. "Because I'm one, too."

The horse neighed nervously, taking a couple steps away to distance herself from their argument –and the saddle.

Joseph dropped the saddle and took two steps toward her. "What do you mean? You're a Wendigo?"

Her lip curled and she nearly burst into tears to hear him say it. It was like his speaking it aloud was what finally made it true, and the realization made her angrier than ever.

She nodded, covering her face with her hands.

"But you're not -"

"I am!" She cried, refusing to let him speak.

"How can that be?"

Cadence slumped down by the fire, overwhelmed by a sense of loss. Joseph would surely leave her now, but she'd promised to be honest. "Because he made me eat Cal's heart."

She pressed the heels of her hands to her eyes. She knew what would come next. Joseph spent all his time helping her hunt this 'Wendigo' only to discover the woman he was protecting was the very monster he hunted? Would he kill her, she wondered?

Did she blame him if he did?

She felt him approach her, but she couldn't take her hands from her face. She didn't want to see the way he looked at her.

"Why didn't you say so?" He asked.

Cadence stifled a sob but steeled herself against the rising anguish she felt. "I didn't want you to know – I think I feared if I told you, then it would be true. And you'd leave me."

The last words cracked in her throat, and she began to sob.

She felt a hand on her head, and she recoiled, fearing the worst. Yet, the touch was soft, and as she turned to meet him, she saw a gentleness to his expression much like the one he'd shown her the night before.

"But you're not sick," he said, as though inspecting her.

She furrowed her brow. "Should I be?"

Joseph smiled. "I don't know. Most men who choose to become Wendigo – well, they change."

"I didn't choose this," she snapped. "He made me. I didn't damn well choose this."

Her words began to deteriorate into soft cries again.

Joseph turned back toward the wood, leaving her slumped under the sliver of a crescent moon. When she finally settled enough to look at him, he was busy putting the saddle on the horse.

Oh god, she thought. He's still leaving.

Cadence stood up, reaching for him as he tied the saddle around the horse's belly. "Please don't leave me. I'm sorry I didn't tell you! I just – you were all I had. I didn't want to drive you away, and I knew if you knew what I was, you'd -"

Joseph's arm was around her waist and his lips were on hers before she could finish. She stiffened in his arms, feeling a strange warmth shoot through every inch of her as his lips found hers. His arms were strong but gentle, and he held her there a long moment, letting her collapse slowly into him. When he finally released her, looking down at her with his warm, brown eyes, she couldn't find words to speak.

"I'm with you, Cadence, but we have to go."

She swallowed, steadying herself as he released his hold on her. "Why? Where must we go?"

He fastened the last strap on the saddle and turned to collect the furs. "I have to kill Shannon Bell."

She swallowed, frantic suddenly at these words. "What? Why?"

Joseph shook his head. "I wish you'd told me sooner. We could've put him out of his misery long ago."

"I don't understand. I thought we were going to catch him? Make him confess or something."

"There's no time for that. You've eaten from the same man's heart. You share a connection that only death can break."

"What?!" She said, the word cracking in her throat.

"No wonder we've crossed his path again and again. You two are connected. He will always be able to find you. Always be drawn in your direction, and you to him. Idiot doesn't even know what he's doing. As long as he lives, you won't be safe."

She opened her mouth to speak, but the words didn't come. After everything that had happened, how could she still be worried for Shannon? 'He promised he'd never hurt me' would sound more than pathetic now.

He seemed to notice her trepidation. He reached out, running his hand down her arm. "You both carry a piece of the same man. You both carry the same essence. You are connected, yes, but you share the power that pulsed in Calvin Hoover's heart. When he realizes that, he may try to kill you to collect the rest."

"Why hasn't he yet, then? And why - he *made* me eat it."

Joseph stopped. "Did you not try to make yourself sick afterward?"

Cadence frowned. "I did. I couldn't do it."

He turned his attention back to strapping down the saddlebags, shaking his head. "Don't worry. You're safe. You're safe with me," he said.

Clearly, her expression betrayed worry. She was glad it didn't betray more.

Joseph slumped down to his satchel and pulled out a small leather bundle. He was leaving their dinner uncooked by the fire.

Cadence recognized the bundle and took it from him, unfolding it to grab a piece of the jerky from within. She let him have it back and he took a pinch.

He helped her up on the horse, handing her the second fur hide before climbing up himself. He reached back and took her arm, pulling it around his middle. The gesture felt intimate now and feeling his body in her arms had changed as well. She knew this man's kiss. She'd felt affection from him like nothing she'd ever felt from a man before.

Yet, Shannon Bell haunted her mind. Affection, she knew now, was no true measure of a man's worth. Affection could be a pretense. It could harbor darkness at its center.

Still, Joseph's breathing didn't feel dark at all as he cooed to the horse gently, leading her back out into the darkness of the plains.

They rode for a long and silent moment before her thoughts demanded a voice.

"Does that make me a Wendigo, too?" She asked, finally. She'd been pained to say the word, not wanting to hear the answer.

He shot her a look over his shoulder. "Perhaps."

She turned her eyes to the stars overhead. "What does that mean? What will become of me?"

The horse's relaxed gait swayed them from side to side as she meandered down the easy slope. "I don't know. You're not hunting for your next meal. If the Wendigo sickness had set in, you'd be searching for the most powerful thing you could find. Like he is." Joseph paused, looking up at the sky for a long moment. "I guess we shall see," he said, finally.

Cadence remembered Shannon's words the night Calvin died.

'No one will ever compel you again,' Shannon had said.

She gave a frustrated half laugh.

How wrong he was, she thought.

The thought of Shannon out there hunting for another victim gave her pause. She glanced over her shoulder toward the trees as they grew smaller in the distance. She tightened her hold around Joseph's body, feeling him groan. She wanted to be warmed against the cold air, as though Shannon Bell himself lingered all around them, watching.

They traveled in silence, the sounds of critters and crawly things in the grass all around them. Had she a calmer heart and mind, Cadence might have found it soothing.

After hours of quiet travel, Cadence began to feel uneasy, a strange pull drawing her forward. She straightened in the saddle to look over Joseph's shoulder.

She gasped softly at the lights up ahead. The pull of familiarity startled her, but with it came abject terror. She loosened her hold on Joseph, leaning back as though preparing to jump off the horse and run for it. He turned to catch a glimpse of her.

"It's alright. It's late. No one will be venturing beyond the outskirts of the city."

"I can't be here, Joseph. How could you bring me back here?"

He reached back and squeezed her thigh. "Shannon and I have a mutual friend in the city. I'm hoping his presence might draw Shannon out."

Her stomach was in knots. Sadly, no reassurance could shake the memory of Sheriff Sharples' look the morning she found Cecil Tennet dead in his office. Finding Cecil Tennet dead wasn't a fond memory either.

"What will you do if Shannon comes?"

"Kill him."

For an instant, the notion hurt her heart. She was protesting the mere idea of there being a connection between herself and Shannon, but each time Joseph said it her heart leapt for an instant. It wasn't because she wanted him – he murdered everyone she cared about. Still, in those milliseconds before she recalled the horror Shannon brought to her life, she grieved him like an ex-lover.

It took only a second for the brutal force of reality to crash over her like some tidal event.

Cadence frowned and held Joseph a bit tighter.

The muscles in her jaw tensed, but she pressed her cheek to Joseph's shoulder and hid her face from the sight of Cheyenne.

The city was deathly quiet. Cadence felt a tinge of gratification knowing that part of that silence was due to her absence. Cheyenne had lost the best saloon in town and one less way to get the ranchers and miners into the city to spend their money. Joseph left her in the wooded tree line on the outskirts of town. Then he marched into the city to do his errand alone.

"It should not be too dangerous, here. Stay in among the trees, keep the hides up around your hair and shoulders. There is no one out at this hour," Joseph said, taking a long route around the quieter corners of the city. When he finally left her to go on the search for his friend, it was well past midnight.

Cadence had certainly considered doing as he asked – but the consideration was short lived.

Cadence marched down the familiar side streets, keeping the fur hide around her shoulders like some primitive shawl, and ducked her head around each corner before stepping out into the streets.

The barber shop, Malcolm Green's office, even the jail was dark as she slipped down the street toward the place she'd once called home. Cadence kept to the muddy street, letting her leather shoes slosh in the mud to avoid making a sound on the wood boards of the sidewalks. She reached the corner of her familiar road and turned toward the Red Onion.

It was eerie to see it so dark up ahead, its front porch cleared of chairs or signs of anyone having done business there. She glanced behind her, almost half expecting Joseph to appear, a look of stern disappointment on his face. Still, she marched out into the middle of the road, tucking the fur up around her ears. She crossed the street to look at her saloon in its full glory.

The windows were covered in paper posters, dingy, tan paper shielding the dark within. Her brow furrowed and she took a step closer to the saloon, her shoulders creeping up to her ears. The posters had so many small words, she couldn't make out half of it, but right at the center of each poster was a word in print so great, she was sure they could see it from Colorado.

AUCTION.

Cadence forgot whatever caution Joseph begged of her and marched up onto the deck of the Red Onion to read the fine print.

Bank owned property. Sale by Auction to be held on the morning of Saturday, March 24th.

Cadence felt her stomach drop through the floorboards beneath her feet.

"No, god damn it," she whispered, touching her hand to the glass as though she might rip the posters down from the outside.

She crossed the deck and tried to open the front door of the saloon – locked.

Cadence took a step back, startling at the sound of someone hooting in the distance. Clearly, the Broken Barrel saloon was still open for business. She could only imagine what a great take they had while her far superior establishment was shut up tight.

She tried the door again as though sheer will might unlock it, but the door did not move.

She pressed her hands to the small sliver of clear glass between the posters, trying to get a glimpse inside, but it was pitch black; there was nothing to see.

Cadence let the fur hide fall, clutching it in her fingers as she rounded the corner of the saloon and headed down the side alley. The door to the back of the saloon was there, the same place where the mining foreman had threatened her with a knife and her dear Joseph had stepped in to save her.

She marched up to the door and tugged at the knob. It too didn't budge.

Cadence curled her fist into the fur hide and felt her jaw clench just as she thrust her wrapped fist into the glass of the door window. The window blinds flapped and folded from the sudden movement, helping to deaden the sound of glass scattering across the floor inside.

Cadence reached through the broken window and turned the lock. The back door to her saloon opened, and she felt a surge of cold certainty race down her back.

This was her home. This was familiar. Yet it felt as though there was nowhere on earth she was less welcome.

Cadence slipped into the back of the saloon, shutting the door quietly behind her, and marched into the bar. The tables and chairs were all rearranged, collected into one corner with the chairs all set atop the tables. The stage curtain was gone now, as was the piano where her friend Maxwell had sat with her many nights, teaching simple tunes – the only ones he knew. Cadence's eyes darted to the floor, scanning the place where once Calvin and Persephone lay, slaughtered like a steer. The floor boards looked as they always had, only the marks of chair legs gouged into them.

Cadence stood in the saloon for a long moment, feeling the emptiness of the space like some breathing thing. Behind the counter, the bottles and glasses were all out of place or missing entirely.

They stripped the place like a bunch of fucking vultures, she thought. A moment later, panic sparked in her chest.

What else had they scavenged?

She darted back down the dark hallway and up the stairs. The upstairs was pitch black, no more than a sliver of the moon outside to offer light. Cadence rushed down the hall toward her bedroom and stood beneath the remnants of the beam where once Abigail hanged herself. Cadence took a moment to push the thought from mind and threw open the door.

Her breath caught in her throat. Though the bed frame, chifforobe, and vanity remained, her personal affects – brush, comb, music box – were all gone. She felt her throat growing tight as she surged across the room, shoving the bedframe aside. She dropped to her knees into the corner of the room and flung the fur aside to give her free movement.

She bent into the corner and dug her fingers under the sideboard, fighting to pry a fingertip between the wood panel and the wall. She felt her fingernail bend back just a hair and hissed, pulling her hand away to relieve the unnerving sensation. She reached for the vanity, opening the drawers in search of something, anything that might work. A long lace hook still remained in the draw, metal from handle to tip.

This would do, she thought.

Cadence leaned back down to the baseboard and jammed the metal hook into the crack between the wall and the wood. The wood shifted. She jammed it down harder, and the wood popped out of the wall, leaving the dark crevice behind it open. Cadence flung the wood aside, ignoring the clattering echo of it as she reached into the small cubby hole. The old cigar box was still there.

She snatched it out of its hiding place and pressed it to her chest, silently thanking the gods.

"Is somebody up there?"

Cadence froze to the sound of the male voice downstairs.

"You ain't supposed to be up here, whoever you are! Come on down or I'll call the Marshal."

Cadence lunged up from the floor, clinging to the cigar box as she snatched up the fur hide and wrapped it around her shoulders again.

There was no hiding behind it now, she thought.

She moved as quickly and silently as she could, frantically trying to imagine a place to hide.

"Don't make me come up there after ya!" The voice called. The man's tone wavered just slightly, and Cadence began to think this man was young – not a hardened guard or thug, as she'd first thought.

He sounded as though he was just as afraid as she was.

The floorboards creaked at the bottom of the stairs, and Cadence spotted the piece of baseboard laying in the middle of her bedroom. The tiny hiding place where she'd stowed all her most precious possessions was open now, betraying that not only had someone been there, but someone who knew the place well. They would know it was her, and they would know she'd taken something. She dove for the wood piece just as the bottom stairs began to creak under the man's weight.

He was coming.

Cadence pressed the flat board back into place, feeling the nails catch on one side. She pushed harder, her heart pulsing in her ears.

"Come on out now! I've got a weapon."

The wood was jammed, one side jutting out from the other baseboard. She pressed with both hands, holding her breath as she listened to the man's footsteps. She had to hide! Damn it, she had to get out of sight.

Cadence felt rage rising in her chest and slammed her fist into the offending piece of wood. It knocked into place, disappearing against the rest of the baseboard.

"I hear you!" The man called, and now his voice wholly betrayed his fear.

Cadence jumped up from the floor and darted across the hallway into Calvin's old bedroom. His room was in similar disarray to hers. She tightened her grip around her prize and frowned.

Rifling through a dead man's things was a whole different kind of wrong, she thought, but she didn't have time to be angry.

She had to be quiet.

She had to be invisible.

"I know you're up here. You might as well just come out!"

The man was at the top of the stairs now. Cadence pressed herself behind Calvin's bedroom door, praying the man would just glance inside and be satisfied, letting fear drive him to go get others before he attempted a deeper investigation.

"Probably just some foolish kids. If you come out now, I won't tell the Sheriff why the back window's broke."

Cadence heard the floorboards just outside the door creak. He was less than two feet away. She swallowed and held her breath.

"Ain't nothing here worth having, boys. Just come on out."

The man was moving into her bedroom now, moving with a cautious gait. She heard her chifforobe doors open and close, then the footsteps moved back into the hallway.

"I know you're here," he said, his voice growing louder. He was just outside the door. Cadence shut her eyes tight.

The man was coming in.

She felt the door press against her feet as the man stepped into Calvin's bedroom. He was moving across the room slowly, but he was far enough in to put her in danger. If the door swung back at all, she'd be visible. He'd turn around and see her. She clamped her eyes shut, praying he'd somehow miss the sight of her.

Don't see. Don't see me! Don't see me! Don't see me!

She stood there silently chanting to herself as the footsteps moved around the room, as though she might magically will herself invisible – or at the very least will him blind. It was a dark night, he didn't have a candle. Please God, she thought.

Don't see me. Don't you see me, you son of a bitch!

The man gasped and Cadence's eyes opened wide, meeting the man's gaze. Her stomach shot into her throat. He was standing in the middle of the room, a curly red haired, young man, no more than twenty, staring at her with his mouth agape. She froze, unable to run or scream or fight. She'd seen him before – retching in the saloon downstairs on the morning they came to find Calvin and her friends in pieces.

He stared at her, his face going white. He seemed just as desperate to run as she was.

The door continued to swing away from her at an agonizingly slow pace. She was caught. There was no sense in holding her breath any longer.

"You – You," he said, his words coming in barely a whisper. "You can't be here. You're dead!"

Dead? She thought. Her brow furrowed and she exhaled. The gesture sent the young man bellowing down the hallway and from the sound of it, stumbling down the stairs.

Cadence didn't dare move at first, listening to the man scramble and scream for help.

Finally, as the sound faded in the distance, she took the opportunity to follow suit. His voice began to echo in the distance. Wherever he was going, he was no longer in or even near the Red Onion.

Cadence rushed down the stairs and along the back hall, ducking her head out into the alley to be sure the coast was clear. When no one appeared to clap her in irons, Cadence dodged down the back alley toward the outskirts of town.

"Cadence?"

Cadence stopped dead at the corner of the Red Onion, staring off toward the trees as though she might pull them closer with her want of them.

"Is that you, girl?"

The voice was soft but strangely familiar. Cadence forced herself brave and turned to find Charlotte standing at the other corner of the Red Onion, glancing back toward the dark road.

"Oh god, Charlotte! Please! Please don't tell. I swear I ain't hurt no one," Cadence whispered in urgency. In the days since finding Persephone and Maxwell dead, Charlotte had hardly crossed her mind. Charlotte was Persephone's closest friend besides Cadence, and she stood there now with a softened expression, glancing behind her every few seconds with the same urgency as Cadence.

Cadence had all but forgotten that Charlotte lived in the rooms above the barber shop.

"They're gonna come lookin for you!" Charlotte whispered as she rushed down the alley toward Cadence. "You gotta get outta here."

"I know. I am! I will!" Cadence said, reaching for Charlotte's hand. Charlotte took it and squeezed, a wordless gesture of trust.

"The law men are out in droves, honey. You gotta stay hidden."

Cadence nodded, turning toward her escape.

Charlotte didn't let go of her hand. Cadence turned to meet Charlotte's gaze.

"What is it?" Cadence asked.

Charlotte frowned. "You swear you didn't do this?"

Cadence felt her face contort in a mix of anger and pain. "You know I didn't, Lotte! You know I didn't!" She said, her voice shaking.

Charlotte squeezed her hand again, pulling Cadence into a rushed embrace. The thought that Charlotte, that anyone that knew her could think her capable of such crimes nearly broke her heart.

"I knew you didn't! I'm sorry! I just – I just had to be sure."

Cadence shook her head, pressing the back of her hand to her eyes as they welled over. "I gotta go," she said, pulling her hand from Charlotte's. She turned down the second side alley and ran, heading for the trees.

"Cadence!"

She glanced back, seeing Charlotte wave as she too fled the scene. "If you get in a fix - come find me," Charlotte called in a fierce whisper.

Cadence's chest felt lighter suddenly as Charlotte disappeared from sight. As distant calls betrayed the return of her witness and whoever he'd managed to rally, Cadence took off down the last few feet of the alley. A moment later she was ducking into the trees, her treasure pressed tight to her chest. Whatever cavalry that young man summoned, she'd be long gone before they arrived. She careened through the trees in the dark, and for the first time in many days, felt a surge of joy.

CHAPTER NINE

"WHAT WAS SO IMPORTANT that you'd put yourself in danger like that, Cadence?"

She sat curled into the furs just as the first light of dawn was creeping across the forest floor. She shook her head. The small cigar box was tucked under her skirts and out of sight, but she could feel the hard corners of it against her thigh. The knowledge of its presence made her calm.

Joseph dropped down before her, forcing her to meet his gaze. "Cadence. I asked you a question."

"I don't like your tone," she said, and the words almost startled her. She shook her head. "I'm sorry you're upset, but I had to. You wouldn't understand."

"You don't know what you've done. What if you'd met with Shannon again? What if he's seen you?"

She swallowed. "He's here?"

"Of course, he is. He is wherever you are. Until he's dead, that will be your world."

"Why would he follow me? He has no reason to!"

"Because he is sick, and whether or not you realize it, you're powerful. More powerful than any man he might choose to take next. He's gonna realize that, and there will be nowhere for you to hide."

"I ain't powerful. There ain't nothing powerful about me!"

Joseph glared at her, a look of exasperation and bewilderment on his face. "You're like him. You may not know how to use that power yet, but when you learn -"

"I'm nothing like him," she said, and the words moved through her like the hiss from a snake.

"Damn it, I can't protect you if you don't do as I say!"

Cadence took a breath, ready to argue right back, but the expression on Joseph's face stopped her before she could utter a word. She watched him a moment, his brow furrowed in concern.

"I'm sorry," she said finally.

He met her gaze, then after a long moment, nodded. "It's alright. Just worries me that you'll run off like that and next time we won't be so lucky."

She stared at the dying embers of their fire, listening to early morning birds chirping in response to the coming dawn. Cadence shifted in her warm cocoon, pulling the box from under her thigh. "Would you like to see what I -"

Joseph shot up to his feet just as a burst of sound echoed through the trees. Men hollered to one another as they moved, the clang of holsters and boots careening toward them, too fast to escape.

Joseph lunged down to her, grabbing her under the arms and hauling her to her feet. She nearly lost hold of the cigar box as Joseph pressed his hunting knife into her hands and turned her toward the trees and shoved her. “Run,” he whispered, his brown eyes wide with worry.

Cadence held a hand out to protest, coaxing him to follow, but he turned away from her, heading toward the sound of the men’s voices.

“Oi! He’s up ahead, Sheriff!”

Cadence ran into the brush, dodging behind the trees to sink low to the ground. She found the darkest shadows she could.

“Can I help you, fellas?” Joseph asked. Cadence could hear the footsteps and heavy breathing. There were at least half a dozen men now in their campsite.

“Well now, Jesse. Here’s your ghost.”

A couple men began to laugh, but one voice among the rest rose up.

“No, it ain’t. I swear to you, Sheriff. That ain’t who I saw!”

The voice that followed was familiar, and Cadence half wanted to burst from her hiding space just for the satisfaction of punching Sheriff Sharples in the nose.

“Come on now, boy. Where were you this evening, if we might pester you with a question?”

“I was here at my camp,” Joseph said, and his voice shuddered mid-speech, as though someone was shaking him as he spoke.

“Is that so? See, we got reason to think you might be lying to us, boy.”

“I am not lying,” Joseph said so calmly, Cadence’s heartbeat almost slowed. Almost.

“Well, see – we had a bit of a break-in down at the Red Onion saloon, and Jesse here thinks he saw a man upstairs in one of the bedrooms. You wouldn’t have any reason to be snoopin around the old saloon, would ya, Eagle Feather?”

One or two of the men laughed at this. Cadence seethed.

Cadence ducked her head around the tree trunk to look and saw the young man from the saloon, his lanky frame smaller now, as though he shrank in the Sheriff's presence. "I'm tellin you Sheriff, that ain't who I saw. It were Ca -"

"That's enough now, Jesse. I don't want to hear any more of it. Tell me, boy. You wouldn't by any chance know a Cadence Delacouer, would you?"

There was a long pause before Joseph spoke. "I do not."

"Now you quite sure about that? You sure it wasn't her that asked you to break in down the saloon, maybe rifle around for some old effects or what not?"

"I said no."

The sound that followed was that of air being expelled from Joseph's chest as someone punched him in the gut. Cadence closed her eyes tight, feeling the overwhelming urge to scream or cry. She felt so helpless there, listening to poor Joseph being harassed by the men who'd forced her from her home. Still, if they knew Joseph was with her, they'd likely do far worse than gut punch him.

"Well, maybe we got it all wrong, huh boy? Maybe you know something about the recent murders down the Red Onion. Maybe Cadence isn't our culprit at all."

She could hear the subtle sound of Joseph chuckling. "Maybe the county should stop deputizing morons."

Cadence gasped just as Joseph was hit again.

Damn it, Joseph! Why would you say something like that?

"Guess we'll have to take you in, then. Give you a night or two in a jail cell to think on it. We got a poster of good ol' Cadence you can have a look at, see if that might jog your memory. Bring him along boys. Try not to damage him too badly."

There were a few grunts and the sound of a tussle, but a moment later, Cadence listened as the men dragged Joseph through the woods towards town, laughing as they went.

"Ya can't go down the jail, Cady. They'll see you and haul you in there, too! Then what good can you do?"

Cadence shook her head, ignoring Charlotte's use of the word 'Cady.' There was no time to correct her. She had to help Joseph.

"I don't have any choice. He's innocent. If I go down and turn myself in, they'll have to let him go. They'll know he wasn't involved."

"But neither were you!" Charlotte said, pacing her small room as the city teemed with life outside. It was past noon now, and Cadence had only just managed to make it into the center of town without being noticed or recognized.

"It don't matter. He's native. There's no way they're gonna treat him fair. No way in hell."

Cadence rose from the edge of Charlotte's bed and snatched one of Charlotte's shawls down from the hook behind her bedroom door.

Charlotte snatched the tasseled end and pulled, nearly ripping the fabric in half. "I said no, Cadence. You can't go. I'm not letting you go."

"You've no power to -"

"Let me go instead. I'll tell em I didn't see no native man that night. They'll believe me if I tell them I live right across the way."

Cadence stopped and stared at her friend. "You'll tell them that?"

"Sure, why not?"

Cadence took a step back from Charlotte, her heart creeping up into her throat. Joseph had said the Sheriff was looking for her because an eye witness came forward with information – a witness whose named she'd burned into memory.

"Was it you? Were you Clairmont? The one who told them I murdered Calvin?"

Charlotte's blue eyes went wide, and her youth played on her face. Charlotte was at least five years younger than Cadence and far shorter on life experience to boot.

"No, Cady! I would never do that! I didn't see anything that night, but if they got your friend in there, what would it hurt?"

Cadence shook her head. "No. It'll look too convenient. They'll probably start suspectin you, with my luck. It's gotta be me. I gotta get down there -"

"Just let me go down and see what they're up to. It'll only be an hour at the most. I'll come right back and let you know what I see. Then you can decide whether you want to go turn yourself in. Alright? Please say alright, Cady."

Cadence watched Charlotte's pleading eyes for a long moment. She would agree. What choice did she really have?

Cadence took a deep breath and exhaled, defeated. "Please call me Cadence, Charlotte."

Charlotte nodded in apology as she wrapped her shawl around her shoulders. "Of course, Cadence. I'm sorry I keep forgetting to."

With that, Charlotte disappeared out into the hallway of the boarding house and disappeared out the front door, the glass in the window frames shaking as she went.

Cadence couldn't tear herself from the window, watching until Charlotte was long gone from view. She waited there a long time, watching the people milling below. The street below wasn't teeming as it normally would by that time of day. Perhaps word of Cecil's murder was keeping people at home.

Cadence watched as a middle aged couple walked down the sidewalk across the way. They were well-to-do, the woman holding tight to a parasol to shield herself from the sun as her husband tipped his hat to passersby.

He made a point to nod to a coatless man as they passed. The man paid them no mind, his face turned toward the boarding house windows. Cadence pulled the shawl down from around her face, pressing closer to the window to see the man.

His eyes went right through her, a grin traveling across his face before she could dodge back into the shadows. Cadence swallowed, watching Shannon stand there as still as stone, staring up at her window.

How had he known to look for her there? How had he found her? Did he hurt Charlotte? Had she led him there?

Joseph's words instantly came to mind.

As long as he's alive, you will always be in danger. Wherever you are, he will be.

The devil's work, she thought.

She watched him for a long moment, the stillness of his stare giving her a hollow feeling in her belly. Finally, he moved, stepping out into the muddy street. Cadence shot forward, pressing her face to the glass to watch him as he crossed the street. He was coming toward her. She turned from the window and rushed for the door to Charlotte's room, barreling out into the hallway with no concern for who might see her. She ran down the stairs scanning the front rooms for a second exit. The back of the house was closed tight, all the doors leading to the landlord's apartments or the barber shop. If he was coming in, she was trapped.

Without thinking, she lunged for the front door, letting the whole house shake as she swung it open to meet him.

There was no one on the porch.

Cadence leaned out, glancing down the road in both directions as though he might lunge out from around the corner.

There was no sign of him anywhere.

Where had he gone?

Worry over her own safety had evaporated. The man who truly killed Calvin was in the city. He was close - if she could find him, perhaps she could cause a scene, expose him.

She stepped out into the muddy street and scanned every direction for a sign of that familiar smirk.

Did she want to turn Shannon in? They'd surely hang him for what he did to Calvin and the others. Did she really want that to happen to him?

It didn't matter what she wanted. He was a Wendigo – this unnatural, insatiable thing, and if anyone deserved to pay for his crimes, she was sure it wasn't Joseph. No matter the affection she'd felt for Shannon, or how much she wanted to believe he was innocent – Joseph *was* innocent, and she knew it. There was no contest.

Cadence turned toward the jail and stumbled, her boot getting caught in the mud. She caught herself just as two gentle hands took hold of her arm.

"Cadence, run!" Charlotte hissed into her ear. "Get inside somewhere. Anywhere!"

Cadence pulled her foot free just in time to meet Charlotte's piercing blue eyes. "What's happening?"

Charlotte shook her head, glancing back toward the jail. "They're coming this way!"

"The Sheriff? Then let them come. Let them take me. I'll tell them Joseph had nothing to -"

"Joseph's been released! Get somewhere quick!"

"He's free?! He'll be back at camp! He'll be wondering where I am!"

"No time! Their heading to Mr. Green's. They're passing this way! Get inside," she hissed one more time, then released her hold on Cadence's arm to walk away, looking as innocent as she could. Cadence glanced back down the road and saw Charlotte was telling the truth. Sheriff Sharples was making his way down the sidewalk with the Detective from out East.

Cadence stumbled back, the mud seeping through to her cold feet, but she did as she was told, careening through the mud toward the closest buildings. Cadence ducked down the nearest alley and instantly recognized the Red Onion's back door, the broken glass in the door now covered with a thin wooden board. She wasted no time, wedging her fingers underneath and pulling until the tiny nails began to come free. There were no telling signs of a coming lynch mob, no hollers of angry men. The city sounded as it always did, bustling and busy, but calm.

Cadence leaned into the door and gave the panel of wood another heave. The door jerked in her hands, pulling from her fingertips and breaking two of her fingernails to the quick. She gasped in pain, clutching her fingers in her fist as the door opened and a figure appeared in the darkness. Before she could cry out or turn to run, Shannon took hold of her arm and yanked her inside.

The Red Onion smelled strange now. All the fumes of alcohol were gone, replaced by the musty scent of old newspapers cooking in the sunlight. Shannon moved her along the hallway roughly, pulling her into the main room and releasing her by the bar. She could feel the heat of another in the room and spun around to find Joseph lying on the floor in the center of the saloon, his hands bound behind his back. He glared at her, as though trying to speak without words, but Cadence could only hear the sound of Shannon's breath, slowing as he moved around the bar.

"There ain't a single bottle left in the place? Are ye kiddin me?"

Cadence watched Joseph on the floor, her heart pounding in her chest. She didn't take her eyes from him as she spoke over her shoulder to Shannon. "Second cabinet on the right. It's tucked up underneath."

Shannon gave her a sideways glare, then moved along the bar, dropping down to check her hiding place. The moment Shannon's dark head ducked out of sight, Cadence pulled the hunting knife from her skirts and tossed it onto Joseph's legs. He scrambled as quietly as he could, letting the knife fall between his knees and out of sight.

"You weren't lyin, girlie," Shannon said, whistling his appreciation as he rounded the bar. "Don't see any clean glasses. Guess we'll be drinkin out the bottle."

He popped the top off the bottle of whisky and took a long swig. Then he turned and offered the bottle to her. Cadence shook her head.

"Come on, now. You'll want a little something to loosen you up. This ain't a pretty thing, I'm about to do to our friend, here."

Cadence turned on Shannon, shaking her head. "You can't – you can't hurt him!"

Shannon gave her a sarcastic look. "I sure can, sweetheart. He's been enough trouble to me to deserve it, too."

Cadence moved slowly, sidestepping to stand between Shannon and Joseph, as though she might somehow protect him from this monster. If what Joseph said was true, this man would be powerful beyond her comprehension. He'd taken the hearts of half a dozen men and women, and those were only the victims she knew. He would have their strength, their influence – their very essence now. All *she* had was prayers.

"Please. You can't hurt him, Shannon. I'm begging you. Let him go."

Shannon's eyebrows shot up. "Oh, I like this begging approach. This might work." He moved toward her, giving her a once over, his eyes lingering at her chest. "You're a beautiful woman. I've never met a woman who could claim to be like me. We could rule this world, the two of us. Take what we want, go where we please, fuck when we like."

She cringed, moving closer to Joseph again.

Shannon lunged at her, pulling her back toward the bar. His grip wasn't cruel or hurtful, but he meant it. "There's nothing for you here anymore. But we're alike, you and me. We could keep each other company in a way no one else could. Tell me you wouldn't like that."

Cadence didn't speak. She stared up into Shannon's handsome face, finding him strange and unfamiliar.

"What reason do you have to protect this poor bastard?" He asked, finally.

She took a shaking breath, glancing down at Joseph's dark eyes as she searched for the truth. The truth came with ease. "I love him."

Shannon's light eyes went wide. He whistled appreciatively. "Is that all?"

Shannon's question came with a sly smirk. She swallowed.

"Listen to me, girl. He's not like you and me. He doesn't *want* that hunger you and I feel. I know you feel it. I know you've seen the power you have. Imagine never having a man tell you what to do again. You can't tell me that ain't temptin."

Cadence stared at Shannon, searching his face for a sign of the gentleman she'd found herself so enamored with. He didn't feel powerful now. He felt wrong.

"Joseph has no power over anybody! Nothing to offer you. He's as powerless as me. Hell, moreso – he weren't born white!"

Shannon's eyebrows shot up. "Is that what you think? A brave warrior like this?" Shannon shot Joseph a wide grin. "Come on, Kayboo. Joey-Joe-Joe. Tell her how we know each other."

Cadence turned to look at Joseph. Joseph turned his eyes down and didn't speak.

"Come on, you!" Shannon said, kicking Joseph's booted foot. "Tell her how you offered to help old Packer and me up into the mountains. Tell her how you left us there to fend for ourselves! You was long gone before all hell broke loose, weren't ya?"

Shannon lunged toward Joseph who still sat with his hands tied, his legs splayed out on the floor before him.

"But not before you told old Packer and me all about those Wendigoes of yours. Silly stories, right? Until we were starving up there in the mountains. Tell me, does she know you're the reason I am what I am?"

Cadence reached for Shannon, pulling him back from Joseph. She could see Joseph shrinking away from these accusations. She didn't know what to think, but it was clear these words were true.

"That's enough," she said. "Let him go!"

Shannon turned on her then, taking hold of her by the shoulders. This touch was unlike any she'd felt from him before. This touch was rough. "You're beginning to test my patience, girly."

"Let him go, and I'll stay with you. I'll do whatever you want, just don't hurt him."

Shannon furrowed his brow. "You think I care about you, honey? Sure, you might be fun to have around," he said, reaching down to grab her between the legs. She smacked his hand away twisting out of his reach. "But I got bigger fish to fry."

Shannon turned toward Joseph, pulling a pistol from his belt.

"I am begging you, don't do this!" She cried, her voice rattling the newspapers along every window. She grabbed Shannon's arm, knocking the gun from his hand. He spun around and took her by the throat, pushing her back into the bar. "That's enough, bitch. If you're not with me, might as well take your heart, too."

Cadence's eyes went wide as she began to see spots at the corners of her vision. She shook her head, trying to break his hold, but he was stronger. She beat on his chest, feeling her heart break as she realized she and Joseph would both perish there, and by the man who'd first stirred her heart with his kindness – by the man she'd protected.

She fought to force words out with her last bit of air. "You promised you'd never hurt me," she said.

Shannon laughed in her face, his blue eyes burning into hers. "I'd never say such a thing."

He bent over her suddenly, his expression changing from relish to shock. His grip loosened and Cadence pulled his hand from her throat just as he slumped against the bar. Joseph was behind him now, the hunting knife buried into Shannon's back.

Cadence recoiled from the men, clamoring across the edge of the bar in her attempt to get away. She lost footing and fell back onto the hardwood floor as Joseph pulled the knife out of Shannon's back and plunged it in a second time. Shannon made a breathless sound, and Joseph held him upright, twisting the handle of the blade. The sound of Shannon's flesh tearing hurt Cadence's ears, but she couldn't look away.

Joseph held the man as Shannon's legs began to weaken beneath him. Finally, Joseph pulled the knife from Shannon's side and let him fall to the floor. Shannon lay there, staring at Cadence as his blue eyes went watery, then still.

He was dead.

Joseph moved across the saloon, dropping to his knees before her. "Are you alright, Cadence? Did he hurt you badly?"

Cadence pressed her hand to her own throat and shook her head. She felt almost wracked with guilt to see Joseph tied as he was, and by the man she'd repeatedly helped avoid capture. Still, Joseph's doe eyes didn't betray the slightest disdain for her.

"You're sure? Can you stand?" He said.

He held his hand out to her and she rose to her feet, wavering there a moment as a pool of blood began to spread from beneath Shannon's body. She found it almost poetic to see the man lying there bleeding in the exact spot where Calvin perished. She stared at him a long moment, her heart hurting at the sight.

"He can't hurt you, Cadence. Not anymore."

Cadence glanced up at Joseph's concerned face but couldn't hold his gaze. She was ashamed – ashamed that Shannon had managed to feed her lies from the night Calvin died, and that she'd wanted to believe him. Ashamed that despite what he'd made her do, she'd protected him, even thought fondly of him at times. Now as she stared at his body, she wanted to kick him for making such a fool of her.

Above all, she was ashamed that at that very moment, having felt his hand around her throat, having seen how little he truly cared for her - even in that last moment she'd wanted to believe the lies.

"Is there anything left upstairs?" Joseph asked, trying to pull her from her spell.

She shook her head, fighting to focus. "What? Yes? What are you looking for?"

"Blankets? Burlap? Something to wrap him in."

Joseph began to move about, slipping into the back room of the saloon as Cadence stood there dumbfounded. The blood crept across the floorboards toward her.

She struggled to find words. "Wrap him?"

Joseph appeared before her, urgency in his expression, though his voice betrayed only patience. "We need to move him. Get him somewhere far from here."

"But he's the murderer."

Joseph touched his hand to her face, and she closed her eyes. His touch felt warm, just as it did the nights before. For a moment, she felt relief in the memory that not all of her choices had been bad.

"It doesn't matter, petal. I'm an Indian. You're a woman, a wanted murderer. They're not going to listen to either of us if we call them in here to show them I stabbed a white man in the same place Calvin died."

Cadence's mouth fell open as though she meant to protest, but the reality of his warning crashed over her like a biblical flood. She was still wanted. Still wanted and homeless, with no one and nowhere to go.

No one, but Joseph. She couldn't let him get in trouble. Not for her. Not after everything.

"There's nothing up there," she said, finally.

Joseph took off to look on the stage for the old curtains but returned after a few minutes empty handed. "Cadence. Duchess. Look at me."

She did as he asked, but it was as though she stared right through him. She felt burdened with purpose. How could she protect him? What could she do?

Tell the Sheriff it was her. It was all her.

"I'm going to go down the way to the general. I'll pick up some blankets. We'll slip him out of here tonight after dark and head out of town. Cadence? Cadence."

He touched his hand to her chin to turn her to him, inspecting her face with concern. She forced him a nod.

After another moment he was gone, slipping out the back door into the alleyway. Cadence stood there in silence, the papered windows offering little light, even in the late afternoon. The smell of Shannon's body was so familiar, she was pained to think the smell of blood and death could become a familiar thing. She stood in the space, wanting to absorb the comfort of her home one last time, but couldn't. She didn't want her most powerful memory of the Red Onion to be the smell of its floors covered in blood.

She turned toward the bar, clutching her still sore fingers in her fists. Her foot tapped against something on the floor beside her. She stopped.

The hunting knife lay blood soaked at her feet. Without thinking, she bent to pick it up, feeling the tacky wetness of Shannon's blood on the handle.

The smell was overwhelming now, blood now staining her hands. She turned toward Shannon's body and dropped to her knees beside him.

He's feasted on more men than you and I could ever know. He's more powerful than we can imagine.

Joseph's words of warning played softly in her foggy mind as she pushed Shannon onto his back. His blue eyes stared up at the ceiling, lifeless. She pressed her fingers over his eyes. She didn't want to feel him watching her work.

Cadence took a deep breath, and working as quickly as she could, pierced the knife into Shannon's side. His flesh gave way with surprising ease, almost turning her stomach, but she pushed, slicing along his lowest rib. She remembered the way Persephone had been lain out, the way her side was open to the world. Cadence worked quickly, yanking Shannon's shirt aside. Another slice across and she had access to her prize. Despite every sour memory of what Shannon had made her do, a strange fever was rising in her. The sounds of the knife cutting, the smell of his blood – all things that would have turned her stomach before now. Yet as she slipped her hand into Shannon's chest, she wasn't repulsed. Her heart was racing.

She was excited.

This was the hunger Shannon spoke of. This was what it felt like, only rising to the fore when she threatened to satiate it.

She cut up into Shannon's heart and pulled a piece of the man out into the open air. His blood was dripping down her wrists and into the sleeves of her dress, but she didn't care. This was what needed to be done. Whatever power this monster possessed, she would take it from him. She would take what she was owed and do with it everything and anything she could - to protect Joseph.

Cadence placed the piece of Shannon's heart on her tongue and swallowed it in one go.

"I knew I chose the right woman."

Cadence jolted around to the sound of the familiar voice. She was so startled, she scrambled over Shannon's body to distance herself from the source. It wasn't possible. This voice couldn't be coming from a living thing. Yet Cadence turned, her hands slipping in blood as she pushed herself away from the figure, sure some new madness was setting in. Madness was the only possible explanation, because there standing in the hallway of the Red Onion was Shannon Bell.

And he was smiling.

"You're dead!" She screamed, and Shannon lunged across the saloon to her side, his finger pressed to his lips to silence her. She wanted to lash out at him. She still held the hunting knife in her hand, but she couldn't move. One Shannon was lifeless on the floor there. She'd watched the life leave his blue eyes, and yet here he was staring at her with an expression of such affection she could barely breathe.

She met his gaze and stopped, words stilled in her throat. This Shannon was staring at her – with brown eyes.

"You're different," she managed to say.

Shannon just grinned at her.

This was the Shannon from the saloon. This was the Shannon from the river that held her underwater to hide her from her pursuers. She fought with every memory she had of him, of every time he'd looked at her with those soft brown eyes.

Cadence turned her attention back to the corpse and screamed again. The dead man on the floor had changed. His face was no longer Shannon Bell's, but was now some strange bearded man with ruddy hair in a mass of curls around his head. She scrambled backward, losing her hold on the knife as she prayed to simply be free of these visions.

"Cadence, my love. You're alright. You're safe. I won't hurt you."

The words landed like dynamite on her ears. The same words she'd heard so many times, spoken with that same gentle, honest tone. She believed those words every time he'd said them – even as the dark version of him tried to choke the life from her, she remembered and believed those words.

"I don't understand. Your eyes were blue."

"When were my eyes blue?" He asked the way a teacher would ask a learning child. He didn't ask because he wanted to know, he asked because he wanted her to remember.

Cadence searched her memory. She'd seen those blue eyes before, and every time they felt strange. It was only now that she realized why.

"Outside the jail. That day they arrested Packer."

"Yes," he said, waiting for her to go on.

The river? No. He'd looked at her with warmth then. The card game? The night in her bedroom? No...the outpost –

"The barn!" She said, scolding herself as Shannon's look of approval made her heart leap like some child hell bent on being the teacher's pet. But she knew she was right. Shannon had felt wrong outside the jail, wrong in the barn, wrong when he stood in the street outside Charlotte's boarding house. He was wrong because his eyes were blue.

He was wrong because he wasn't Shannon.

Not *her* Shannon, anyway.

"This isn't possible. You're not – possible."

Shannon smiled at her, and it had the same disarming effect it always had. "I can explain, but you must promise me you will not scream."

She stared into his warm brown eyes, the gunpowder voice soft and calming despite everything she'd witnessed. She took a deep, shaking breath and nodded.

"Ok, Cadence. Close your eyes."

Her brow furrowed, as though closing her eyes would leave her more vulnerable than she already was. Shannon just smiled at her, patiently waiting.

She did as he asked, her heart racing in her ears.

"Alright. Open them."

The voice had changed again, and she gasped. She knew what she would see before she opened her eyes. For a moment, she almost couldn't bring herself to do so.

Her mind raced, unwilling to take in what she knew she was about to see.

She took a shaking breath, remembering words spoken only a few moments before. Words spoken, but not by Shannon. "You called me Duchess."

She opened her eyes and held her breath as she met Joseph's gaze – those same beautiful brown eyes staring back at her.

Her Joseph and her Shannon were the same man.

Her throat grew tight. "I don't understand."

Joseph's expression softened - she was growing teary-eyed, and he took hold of her, pulling her across the floor, away from the ruddy haired corpse. Joseph pulled her into his arms, pressing his nose into her hair as he held her. She felt the strangeness of the world like a dream she couldn't wake from, but Joseph's arms felt warm and safe - familiar. Even as the world stopped making sense, she let herself get lost in that embrace for a moment. Perhaps madness wasn't so bad if she had Joseph there at her side.

"I know this must be frightening -" Joseph began, but she stopped him. She wasn't ready to hear anything more.

Cadence stared at the floor, watching the blood creep out from beneath this stranger's body. She took a long time, letting Joseph rock her gently in his arms. When the blood stilled finally, choosing its boundaries around the dead man, Cadence finally spoke.

"Who is he?"

Who is this man whose heart I just cut out? Who is this man with the blue eyes that tried to kill me? Who was this darker version of Shannon Bell?

"That man's name was Frank Miller, but we called him 'Reddy.'

Reddy, she thought. She remembered the nickname from the newspaper that day in the bank. The man's tangles of hair explained the nickname nicely.

"We?" She asked, finding the act of forming words almost too difficult to manage. Her mind was swimming in a mad whirlwind of thoughts. She didn't know which to believe, if it was all symptoms of madness, or whether it mattered. She was beginning to believe madness was all she had to hold onto.

"Alfred and the rest of the group."

Cadence turned up to face Joseph, his tan face still harboring the gentlest smile despite what transpired around them. Cadence didn't speak, waiting for Joseph to offer his explanation.

He took a deep breath, watching her face as he released his hold on her. "I will tell you everything you might want to know, but for now – we have to move the body. I can't take the chance of you being blamed for another murder."

Joseph hopped up from beside her, holding onto her shoulder as he moved to be sure she was steady on her own. She touched his hand, feeling the familiarity of his skin, even as she questioned everything else about him. She watched him hustle across the hardwood floor, tossing a massive sheet over the lifeless form of Frank Miller.

"Did you kill Calvin?"

Joseph stopped, shooting her a patient smile. "No, Duchess."

Cadence exhaled. "So, it was him – Reddy killed all those people?"

Joseph nodded, not looking up as he rolled Miller's corpse onto the sheet. "Almost all of them."

Cadence leaned back at these words, as though she might distance herself from them. "Almost?"

Joseph shot her a sideways look, not breaking from his work. "Cadence, petal. Worry about this later -"

"How can you ask that of me? What do you mean almost?"

Joseph sighed, slumping back onto his haunches a moment. Finally, he exhaled and shot her a wary look.

The second his eyes met hers – that sideways smile that betrayed both mischief and patience, the same one she'd seen so many times on Shannon Bell's face - she remembered that exact look in Shannon's brown eyes as he left the bank.

"You killed Cecil," she said, and the words were barely audible.

Joseph seemed pleased with her, giving a half nod as he returned to wrapping Reddy into his death shroud. "I did. I had no choice."

Cadence looked down at her blood soaked hands, feeling cold all over. "You killed Cecil."

Joseph moved across the floor, taking hold of her stained hands in his own. "He had power over you. Too much power for any man to have over another. I couldn't let that stand. If there was only one man on this earth whose power you deserved, it was his."

"But I gained nothing from his death."

"You gained more than you know," Joseph said, his hand moving to his back pocket. A moment later, he pressed a familiar leather satchel into her palm. The smoked pork that she'd found so delectable in the brush.

She stared at the satchel for a long moment as comprehension settled into her troubled mind. The meat hadn't been smoked pork. It was Cecil Tennet's heart.

"You made me eat the heart of my stepfather. The heart of Cecil Tennet. Why would you do that to me?"

Joseph squeezed her hand so tight, the blood oozed from between her fingers. "I couldn't stand to see you beholden to them like that. I heard Calvin speaking to you that first night – pushing you to dance for your keep. I could hear the fury and the passion in your voice. You deserved to be treated like a queen. Instead, you were pretending to be a barmaid to save your stepfather's face."

"He didn't deserve to die for that."

"No! Of course not. Cadence, you understand that I didn't kill him, don't you?"

She shook her head, a pressure building at her temples as she fought to make sense of everything. "But you are Shannon Bell?"

Joseph dropped low to meet her gaze, only half glancing at the front door when passersby rapped at the papered glass on their midafternoon stroll.

"I am the man you see before you. This is my true self."

"Then who was the real Shannon Bell?"

Joseph frowned. He was agitated. He wanted to be done with the mess that lay across the saloon floor, but his expression still betrayed infinite patience with her. They could be caught there with this corpse, both of their lives ended in an instant, but Cadence couldn't find the strength to stand or help – it was taking all of her strength not to go mad.

"The real Shannon Bell died on the mountain in Colorado."

"But he was here? He was at the river. He *touched* me," she said, and her voice hissed with despair.

"Every kindness and gentle moment you remember of Shannon – that was me, Cadence."

She pointed to the man on the floor, her hand shaking.

Joseph didn't wait for further question. "I met Alfred Packer before they went into the mountains. I tried to help a friend, Chief Ouray, deter them from going on. The mountains are not kind in the cold. I made the mistake of telling them the stories of the Ute – of my own people - the creatures that eat the hearts of men – take their power. They believed them to be myths and went anyway. I offered to take them as far as I could."

Cadence swallowed, remembering the moment she saw Shannon's name in the paper as one of the dead.

"Packer told the truth. When his party got lost and began to starve, he went to find help. He found me. When we returned to his camp, we were too late. Shannon and the rest of his party were dead. Reddy killed them all. The Wendigo sickness had taken him."

Cadence shot a sideways glance at the man now wrapped in a blood soaked sheet.

"Israel had died, and they'd been forced to eat him. Reddy was the only one to eat his heart. He went mad. He was not made for power like that."

Cadence fought to make sense of what she was hearing. "So, he became Shannon Bell?"

"No, no. But that day he took on the essence of Shannon Bell. He carried the essence of everyone he slaughtered. With such power, he could make others do as he commanded – even see something that isn't there. He chose which of his faces you would see. When you looked at Reddy, you saw Shannon because he wanted you to."

"You were Shannon, too..." Cadence said, finally letting herself look Joseph in the eye again. The kindness in his brown eyes made her thoughts still a moment.

"I had no choice, but to follow suit. I knew Reddy would be dangerous. I had to hunt him down before he did more damage. The best way to track him was to share in the same heart as him. If we shared the essence of Shannon Bell, we would be connected. Alfred and I both ate part of Shannon's heart that day."

Cadence thought of the man locked away in a Cheyenne jail cell. "Alfred is like you?"

Joseph stood up again, crossing the room to finish wrapping Reddy's body. "He is – and he isn't. I am what I am by choice. I watched my family murdered, saw my friends taken, beaten, forced to accept the white man's ways with the promise we would be accepted into their world if we did. But that was a lie. They beat our language from us and crushed us under their boots."

Joseph's tone had changed. Patience was faltering in place of anger – an anger she couldn't blame him for. These words were enough to make her angry as well.

"I knew the stories of Wendigo as a child, I knew it could drive me mad – make me a monster, but I made a choice. If there was a chance having this power could help me spare even one child from what was done to me, the risk was worth it. I am not consumed by this power like Reddy was because I wanted it for very different reasons."

Joseph paused, touching the only clean part of his hand to his eyes. Cadence felt her chest growing tight as she listened.

"But Alfred? That man wasn't meant for this kind of power either. It's just not in him. Alfred would give anything to be rid of it. He could have hidden behind Shannon Bell's face any time. Even now, he could be free simply by demanding his release. He refuses."

A burst of noise startled Joseph toward the windows as the silhouettes of people passed by outside, laughing in quiet conversation.

Cadence's thoughts began to clear slowly. "Alfred. He's the friend you came to visit," Cadence said, watching Joseph snatch another long stretch of dark, dusty fabric from the back hall. Joseph nodded his answer, turning his full focus to the work at hand.

He rolled Reddy up and hoisted him over his shoulder, leaving a strange pattern of blood across the floor. Cadence stared across the room, listening to Joseph settling Miller's corpse by the back door. When he returned to view, he was carrying rags. Cadence crawled across the floor, holding her hand out to him in wait of one of them.

Joseph stared down at her, frowning. "You don't need to do this, Cadence. It is my fault he is dead. It is my fault any of this happened to you."

She shook her head. "I cut that man's heart out. I made that choice."

She met his gaze, fighting to settle her nerves and show a brave face. A subtle smile slowly crept across his face. "I know you did. Why?"

She set her jaw, her throat growing tight as she forced out the words. "You were already arrested and released once this week. I feared they wouldn't let you go a second time. I thought if I was powerful enough, I could – I could make them leave you alone."

Joseph's eyes grew darker, and he reached out to touch her face, stopping when he saw the state of his bloodied fingers.

"They didn't let me go, Cadence."

Her eyebrows shot up. "What?"

He shook his head. "I didn't want you to worry, but – they didn't release me. I was left alone with one of the guards. I compelled him to let me go."

Cadence swallowed. "Does that mean -?"

"They still believe I did it. I'm a wanted man."

She didn't speak, but instead held her hand out for a rag. Joseph stared at her for a long moment, wordless. Then, they both set to work cleaning up the blood from Reddy's corpse. Joseph brought a bucket of water from the back room, and the water ran thick with red before they were done.

The light was fading outside by the time they finished. Joseph moved swiftly, his footsteps almost silent as he readied himself for the next step – moving Frank's corpse out of the saloon.

The moment came when Joseph was to leave, and Cadence stood by the bar, staring at her saloon. The only thing to betray what had happened there was the still lingering tinge of copper in the air.

Joseph waited in the back hall for a long time. When Cadence didn't follow, he reappeared, coming up to stand behind her. His presence felt so strange now – like all the pieces of Shannon and all the pieces of Joseph, now rolled into one undeniable force that she couldn't forsake. He touched his clean hands to the small of her back, bringing his nose to her ear. "Are you alright, petal?"

She wasn't sure. The chaos of her thoughts just an hour before had faded, and in the quiet, she could feel something pulsing beneath her skin. Every man that Frank Miller had killed, every heart he'd devoured – she could feel their power in every beat of her own. The confusion and guilt were memories now, and in their wake, she felt a thousand feet tall, fearless – ready. Yet, despite all the power she felt coursing through her, she stood in the center of her greatest grief, the home she could no longer claim. Cadence didn't turn to him, but instead stared at her saloon, feeling her heart ache.

She took a deep breath. "You made me like you to free me, but now - I have nothing."

Joseph kissed the crook of her jaw and pulled her back into him, gently. "We will change that, my queen. We will change it together."

Joseph released his hold on her and offered his hand. Cadence turned to meet him and found Shannon Bell standing before her again. Despite the ache of leaving the only place she'd ever called home, she took his hand and let him lead her to the back door of the saloon.

CHAPTER TEN

THE GREED OF WHITE men can't help but succumb to power like this.

Those were Joseph's words as he prepared her for the morning's affairs.

"But we are not the white men," he said, tucking a strand of her hair behind her ear.

Cadence stood behind the post office, fighting to steady her breath.

"Look at me, Duchess," Joseph said. "You're going to be fine. Now, relax your arms. Remember, walk in there with the confidence of a man. No one will question you."

She furrowed her brow, imagining the way men walked and moved. She loosened her hold on the cigar box, fighting the urge to clutch it to her chest. A man wouldn't fold into himself like that. A man would walk chest out, puffed up like some prancing bird. Cadence glanced down at her chest, now jutting out under her chin. Even Joseph noticed and gave her an eyebrow waggle.

Cadence blushed.

"You'll have them eating out of your hand. You're ready."

Cadence swallowed, straightened her spine, and marched around the corner of the post office.

You see what I want you to see. You see what I want you to see. See what I want you to see.

She chanted the words in her mind, feeling her boots slosh in a shallow puddle as she stepped out onto the main drag. She stepped aside quickly to let a tall man in a bowler hat pass her, then caught herself. Would a man step aside like a gentle little kitten at the mere approach of another man?

No, damn it! Stand up straight, Cadence.

She moved toward the sidewalk, striding along to join the promenade of ladies and their chaperones. Then she caught herself, turning out into the muddy road and stomping through the muck across the intersection toward Malcolm Green's office.

It was taking almost all of her focus just to keep chanting her mantra. Joseph assured her she need only think it once – yet she couldn't fathom that what he said might be true. This was her test. This would prove one way or another if she'd become like Joseph.

Cadence marched up the steps toward the front door of Malcolm's building just as a man in a top hat gave her a curt nod, tapping his finger to the brim of his hat. She stopped a moment, considering the gesture.

Cadence glanced over her shoulder to see Shannon Bell – her Shannon Bell - standing at the corner of the intersection, watching from a fair distance. She sighed, feeling comfort in knowing he was close. If screams and hollers followed her arrival, he'd be there to sneak her away before the deputies arrived.

At least she hoped.

Cadence took hold of the doorknob in her shaking hand, and scolding herself, opened the door.

You see what I want you to see. You see what I damn well want you to see.

Cadence marched up the stairs and stormed into Malcolm Green's reception area, giving his assistant an impatient glare. "Is he in?"

The assistant startled up from his work, met her gaze, then shot up from his seat, knocking the chair half sideways as he moved. "Yes. He's right inside. Come on in."

Cadence watched the young man, his demeanor so different now than last she'd been there.

"Sir. You have a visitor," the assistant said, ducking his head into Green's office.

"Of course, of course. Send them in."

Cadence gripped the cigar box in her right hand as she slipped past the assistant into Malcolm's cluttered office.

"How may I help -" Malcolm said, stopping just as he looked up from his papers. He met Cadence's gaze and his jaw dropped. "My god. Dear god. How are you he -"

Cadence flung the cigar box onto Malcolm's desk, knocking papers and pens askew as it rolled and settled. Malcolm was visibly shaken, as though he were afraid to go near his desk now.

"You've got my saloon up for auction. I'm here to rectify that fact."

"I thought – we all thought you were -"

"You were mistaken. Now, hush up and open the damn box!"

Malcolm searched the desk for his glasses, pulling the bifocals up to his nose to inspect what lay before him. He touched the box as though he half expected a rattlesnake to be hiding inside. Cadence felt satisfaction at such a thought.

"What's this?" Malcolm said, his voice shaking.

"Open it and find out," Cadence said, making a point to sound impatient.

Malcolm swallowed, settling himself in his chair. He turned the frayed paper box over and opened the flap with shaking hands. Three folded pieces of paper unfurled slowly from within. Cadence waited for him to inspect them.

The first was her father's will, leaving the Red Onion to Cadence. The second was her mother's will. The third – the most important piece of the puzzle, was the deed to the Red Onion, with *Cadence Delacouer* clearly written as sole proprietor.

Malcolm stared at it, the paper flitting in his hands.

"Do you need anything further from me?" Cadence asked.

Malcolm shook his head. "No, no. This is quite enough. I'll be in contact with the bank this afternoon."

"Good," she said, leaning in to collect her papers.

"Wait," Malcolm said. She was halfway through stuffing them back into the cigar box before Malcolm spoke again. "It's good to see you well, Cal. We all - we thought you were dead."

Cadence felt a shiver run down her spine. Everything Joseph said was true. This man – every man, woman, and child on the streets of Cheyenne were under her spell. When Cadence walked through the streets, they saw what she wanted them to see.

She turned around, staring at Malcolm Green with a new fury in her heart. This new power she possessed, that allowed her to make commands of those around her – it wasn't this power alone that set Malcolm Green's hands to shaking.

It was because when Malcolm Green looked up from his papers, it wasn't Cadence he saw standing in his office.

It was Calvin Hoover.

"Is it, Mal? Because from what I hear, seeing me is the last thing you want. You're lucky I don't wring your neck for what you did to my girl," Cadence said, emotion rising in her chest. She relished the panic in Malcolm's eyes.

Malcolm recoiled just so, pushing his chair from the desk to distance himself from her. "I had no choice. Cecil's bank wanted the property. There was nothing I could do -"

"Are we done here?" Cadence asked, stepping toward the door, the cigar box clutched in her right hand.

Malcolm nodded. "Yes, of course. I'll have the deed on file with the bank right away."

"You damn well better. I expect to be compensated for every drop of liquor I lost while you and Cecil were diddling around with our property. Do you understand me?

"Well, sir -"

"Otherwise, I'd be happy to let the Sheriff know exactly what the two of you were getting up to before poor Cecil's death. I wonder if that might draw suspicion to you. Tell me, have they found Cecil's killer yet?"

Malcolm's face went white. He shook his head, fumbling for words, but Cadence didn't wait for him to speak.

"Cadence will be down the Red Onion tomorrow. You may deliver compensation to her directly. Oh – and an apology would be a nice touch, wouldn't you say?"

"Of course. Surely, Mr. Hoov -"

Cadence didn't wait for Malcolm Green to finish his words. She felt massive, a giant among men. She glanced at the assistant one last time, giving him a sly smirk as she stormed out of the office and back down the steps toward the main street.

The air outside was thick with the smell of muck and horses, but it smelled like freedom now. She stood on the front steps of Malcolm's office, staring down a tall, top hatted man as he came barreling down the sidewalk toward her. Unlike any other day in her life, she didn't step aside for him. Instead, she glared, daring him to complain about her presence. He marched up toward her, met her gaze and faltered, then tapped the brim of his hat and stepped aside, his boots sloshing in the mud as he walked around her.

Cadence took a deep breath, her chest filling with the dusty air, and she smiled.

The world suddenly felt infinitesimally smaller now. There was nothing she couldn't do or have and once it was hers, there was no man alive who could take it from her.

"Shall I walk you home, m'lady?"

Cadence startled at this but turned to find Shannon Bell standing behind her.

She laughed, catching herself mid giggle. How strange it would look to the rest of the world to see Calvin Hoover giggling like a school girl on the sidewalk with a six foot something man in black.

"Can you see me?" She asked, looking into the familiar warm eyes.

He smiled. "I would recognize those eyes anywhere."

Cadence stiffened a moment, remembering to stand like a man. The instinct to shrink each time a man walked by was ingrained in her so deeply, she felt angry with each tremor of it. She turned to him and shook her head. "I have one more stop I need to make."

To say Sheriff Sharple's was surprised was an understatement. Cadence sat down with the man, relishing in the nervous energy both the Sheriff and Detective Finkbone exhibited as she explained her version of events.

Frank "Reddy" Miller was not dead, as Alfred Packer had confessed, but had come to town looking for trouble, and found it in the Red Onion. After killing two employees and a visitor from out of town, he'd dragged Calvin into the plains, aiming to demand a ransom. Calvin overpowered him after a few days, slit the man's throat, and escaped.

Cadence was nervous telling the story, given it was a bold faced lie, but the words were coming from the mouth of a man they'd thought dead. Whatever they wanted to think, at least Cadence's name was cleared.

Sadly, she couldn't very well clear Joseph's name. Not only was he wanted for Cecil's murder, he'd escaped capture. And he was Indian. Even her word wouldn't be enough to stop the vendetta they had for him.

Shannon Bell waited for her to leave the jail and walked her home.

The musty, yellowed paper was still stuck to the windows, but the light within the Red Onion was enough to work.

Cadence made her way upstairs, a tiny notepad and pencil in hand.

"What's this?" Joseph asked as he joined her in her bedroom.

She stood a little taller. "I'm keeping a tally of everything that is missing. I'm going to be demanding compensation when Malcolm arrives in the morning."

Joseph smiled. "I could get used to this."

Cadence scribbled down the words - *three mattresses, one upright piano, seven tailored dresses.*

"Get used to what?"

"You taking command as you are."

Cadence couldn't fight the smile that overtook her face. "Is that so?"

Joseph sauntered along behind her, glancing into each room as she scribbled words, each one with a little more fervor than the last. Seeing just how little was left of the place was making her furious.

"My god damn slippers? Are you kidding me?" She groaned to herself before finally making her way back downstairs. She watched Joseph come down the stairs with a relaxed gait, then turned toward the daunting task of bar inventory. They'd be replacing enough booze to serve an army, by the looks of it.

"Hope it tasted good, you pricks," she said under her breath.

Joseph stepped close behind her, and she could see his face in the mirror behind the bar. He wrapped his arms around her waist, pulling her into him as she counted the empty spaces along the wall.

She lost count twice, once when he pressed his nose into her hair, and again when he kissed her ear.

"You're gonna be trouble, I see," she said, turning to smile at him.

Joseph gave her a wicked grin. "Tell me, Duchess. Have you ever considered christening the bar?"

Her eyes went wide. "What?"

Joseph gently took the notepad and pencil from her hands and set them on the counter. Then without further explanation, he grabbed her by the waist and hoisted her up onto the long wooden bar. A moment later, he was over her, smiling down as her hair cascaded over the edge.

She stifled a nervous whimper. "What are you doing?"

Joseph reached down and began to tug her skirts up to her waist. She didn't protest, only glancing toward the papered windows in nervous excitement.

"I'm having my way with you. You don't think the owner will mind, do you?"

Cadence laughed, reaching down to unfasten Joseph's britches. She took hold of him in her hand, relishing in the feel of him again, then wrapped her legs around him as he took her on the bar.

The counter was dusty now, all the bottles empty or absent entirely. Cadence tied an apron around her waist and made quick work of pulling the bottles down from the shelves. The dust kicked up with each pass of the rag, but as the moments passed, the brass and mirror found their sheen. Joseph left to deal with Reddy's corpse, leaving her a few hours to clean and put things to sorts.

A dusty grave out in the plains was more than Reddy deserved, she thought. Still, she certainly didn't need him in her wine cellar.

Cadence hauled a few hidden bottles of whisky and bourbon up from her trusted hiding places and beat the dust from the curtains upstairs. Despite there being no mattresses, she wasn't too concerned. She'd become accustomed to sleeping in the brush. She was sure they could make the floor comfortable enough for the time being.

Cadence worked for hours, feeling a lightness to her step. With each brush of the rag and every sneeze the dust drew, she felt at peace.

This was hers.

And that was hers.

Even the half dozen dead moths in the lamp cover were hers. It all made her smile. And with no less relish, with each passing moment, she knew Joseph would be back soon. Chairs had been knocked about since she was last there, leaving a few in need of some tending. She fished a hammer and some nails out from the back room to set chair and table legs. She was almost done rearranging the saloon by the time there was a knock at the door. She smiled.

"Come on in. I left it open," she called as she hopped up onto the stage to sweep up the footprints left in the dust.

The bell over the door jangled as he entered the saloon. She didn't look up from her work.

"I just had to see it for myself."

Cadence jumped. This voice didn't belong to Joseph – or Shannon. Yet, she recognized it all the same.

She looked up to find a familiar face glaring at her from the front door of the saloon. The mining foreman – the man who'd cornered her in the back alley – who'd threatened her with sour breath, and dark intentions – was standing in the middle of the Red Onion, leering up at her from beneath his mass of dark hair.

"You should be strung up by now, bitch."

She stared at him, suddenly aware of how alone she was. "You get out of here. We ain't open yet, and even if we were, you know you're not welcome here."

"Oh, I've no intention of leaving. God damn it! How are you not in jail?"

She furrowed her brow. "Because I ain't done nothing!"

The mining foreman moved closer to the stage. Cadence quickly hustled to the edge, plotting her escape. The stage had no back exit. If she jumped now, she could make it to the back door. If she stayed put, he'd corner her there, and she'd be helpless.

"Ain't done nothing, huh?"

"Get out! Help!" She screamed, turning her eyes to the still papered windows. Her heart dropped into her stomach. If she and Joseph had simply taken down the papers, someone might see her – know she was there. Instead, they'd left them up for privacy, and potentially sealed her fate.

"Ain't no one coming for you, girlie. I don't know how you managed this, but I won't let it stand. I'm not letting some foul whore make a fool outta me."

Cadence ran to the edge of the stage and jumped down, barreling between chairs and tables to get away from him. Yet the foreman was too quick, catching her by the arm just feet from one of her still broken chairs.

"I tried to do this the nice way. If the Sheriff had just come and taken you in, we wouldn't be havin this trouble."

She could smell his breath now, and the memory of that night in the alley flooded her mind all over again. She wanted to get away from him, but it felt as though he slithered into her space from every direction.

"Please stop," she pleaded in barely a whisper.

"I told that Sheriff what I saw. Gave him all manner of details. It shoulda been enough. How'd you get out of it? You tell me right now, and maybe I'll go easy on you."

Cadence turned to meet his gaze, her eyes wide. "You did what?"

He smiled, betraying a blackened tooth at the corner of his mouth. "*Oh, Sheriff. I saw it all. She was a madwoman. Cut em all up into pieces. I saw everything through the window. Saw it all,*" The foreman said, putting on a high pitched, frightened tone. "He bought every bit of it."

Cadence jerked in his grip, trying to pull her arms free. She remembered the wanted poster – Joseph warning her that they were coming for her – that an eyewitness account was the break in the case they needed. Cadence glared up into the face of her captor and felt a new rage burning in her gut. She remembered the witness' name. "You're Matthew Clairmont?"

He grinned. "I do love that they put me in the paper and all. Had a grand old time down the mines with everyone askin for details. I assure you, I let my imagination run wild. You'd be surprised how easy it is to spin a tale like that."

Cadence turned toward the nearby table, planting her hand over the handle of her hammer, and swung it back into the foreman's face. The hammer made brutal contact with his cheek, and Matthew Clairmont's face went slack instantly. He lunged back, drawing up his arms to shield himself, grabbing her by the wrist to stop her from swinging again. She tried to yank her hand from his grasp, but he held strong.

"Let go of me, you son of a bitch!" She growled in his face.

He did as she demanded, his eyes growing wide with surprise and fear.

Cadence stood stock still a moment as the two of them stared frozen in the realization of what had happened. Cadence swallowed, still holding the hammer up over Matthew's head.

She'd compelled him. She'd commanded him and he'd done exactly as she asked, without a second's pause. She'd forgotten this power she possessed. The revelation of it surged in her chest, and she stood just an inch or two taller.

Matthew stared at her, his mouth open. "How in the hell -?"

"Get away from me," she said, her words now as calm as the surface of a still pond. Matthew's face contorted in confusion and fear, but he did as she said, taking two steps away.

Cadence let her hand fall to her side, the hammer hitting her thigh with a light tap. She stared at him a long moment before his panic stricken expression faded.

He turned for the door. "We'll see how tough you are next time, you fuckin witch!"

"Stop!" She said.

Yet again, Matthew Clairmont did as he was told. Cadence stood there in the quiet space of her saloon and fought with the excitement she felt. This man – the man who'd almost lost her everything – the man who'd threatened her, hurt her, leered at her, and lied about her was now helpless in the wake of her word. Despite Joseph's assurances that she was and would never be a power hungry, greed driven creature like the Wendigoes of his people's stories, at that very moment, she felt giddy with the power she wielded.

Matthew Clairmont couldn't frighten her now, no matter how strong a grip he might have.

"Come back here," she said, stepping toward him. Matthew's eyes were wide and wet, but his body moved nonetheless, coming to stand just before her.

She glared up into his dusty, coal stained face, his left eye swelling near shut from the hammer as he waited for her to speak again.

"Get on your knees," she said.

Matthew dropped onto the hardwood, his knees making a loud thud that echoed through the empty space.

"Cadence? What are you doing, petal?"

Cadence turned to find Joseph standing by the back hallway watching her. She met his gaze, his look of worry giving her only an instant's pause. Then without another word, Cadence raised the hammer high over her head and smashed it down onto the top of Matthew Clairmont's skull. The man dropped onto the hardwood like a sack of dusty potatoes, a halo of blood spreading around him.

She stood there in the silent saloon, waiting for Joseph to speak. She waited for his disdain, for his utter rejection of her. She knew this deed to be dark, but in the moment when Matthew Clairmont leered at her, Cadence saw every man that had ever forced their will on her. Every hand up her skirt, every oppression, every violation – they'd all come flooding to the fore. She'd known that powerlessness too many times.

She would never allow another man to make her feel that way again.

Cadence finally turned to meet Joseph's worried look. Yet, his expression had changed. Those warm eyes didn't betray worry or disapproval. He looked at her with the same passionate acceptance he had as they lay across her bar after making love.

Joseph met her gaze and shrugged. "Guess I'll bring the cart back around. You're cleaning up the blood this time."

EPILOGUE

Cadence stood at the window of her rented bedroom and watched the quiet stretch of road outside. There were no signs of anyone in the street below. Even the rest of the house was quiet. She was sure the chill of the February air kept the average person tucked indoors, nestled by their fires with their families.

Still, Cadence could not sleep until she knew Joseph was home safe with her. She simply couldn't sleep alone anymore.

There was a rustle across the bedroom. She froze, listening for further sound, but nothing came. She exhaled and continued to watch outside.

Her breath gathered on the glass, fogging her view as the silhouette of a carriage appeared in the road below. Cadence took a sharp breath and moved as soundlessly as she could across the Oriental rug, her bare feet padding along in near silence.

In the hallway below, the front door opened with a blast of cold air, sending the hanging crystals on the chandelier to clink against one another. Despite her state of near undress, Cadence rushed down the stairs and stopped on the last step, waiting for Joseph to acknowledge her. The tall man in the wide brimmed hat looked up at her and smiled, the familiar warmth of Joseph's eyes framed perfectly by Shannon Bell's handsome face. Cadence smiled back at him. She'd grown accustomed to loving this face as much as she loved Joseph's true face. Sadly, a white woman married to a native man wasn't the most acceptable coupling in modern society.

Especially when that native man is wanted for the murder of a Cheyenne banker.

After a long moment of simply greeting Joseph with a lingering look, the second man stomped his feet on the front stoop, blowing air out through pursed lips to express his chagrin with the cold. Cadence turned to greet the second man, nodding in friendly welcome.

"Hello, Alfred. It's nice to finally meet you."

The older man beamed at her, his bushy mustache almost completely hiding his teeth from view. He tipped a non-existent hat at her, his demeanor still somewhat excitable. She could understand his high energy. This was the first day Alfred Packer had spent outside a prison in nineteen years.

"Thank you, ma'am. This is quite the place you've got here," he offered, whistling in appreciation as he inspected the room.

Cadence smiled politely. This wasn't her home. Still, she'd paid the rent, it was hers for the few nights they would be in town.

Cadence glanced upstairs, keeping an ear open as she crossed to the bookshelves. "Would you like a drink, Mr. Packer? Or perhaps something to eat. We had a lovely venison for supper. I'm sure there's some left -"

"Oh no, no," he said, pressing his hand to his belly. "I'm quite fine, thank you kindly."

Joseph pulled the hat off of his head and his long black hair unfolded down his back in a perfect braid. He didn't need to hide his true face from Alfred. They were old friends by now.

"You look to be doing quite well for yourself there, Joe," Alfred said, accepting the glass of bourbon that Cadence offered. She smiled at this, letting Joseph respond to his compliment.

She and Joseph had done very well for themselves. Despite Joseph's native birth, he'd lived much of the last nineteen years as one Shannon Bell, becoming a respected businessman in Cheyenne. He and his wife kept a reputation for discerning taste and wise investing. As a result, Cadence's family name was now plastered across half a dozen businesses throughout Cheyenne. Yet, as the years passed, they soon outgrew the close-knit community of Cheyenne. There were only so many times a woman could profess to simply aging well as the decades passed and Cadence's face didn't change. Shannon Bell remained equally rugged and youthful. It was only a matter of time before someone noticed and stories began to spread.

Cadence crossed toward the front door, glancing out into the cold for a sign of life. There was still nothing there. The two men were conversing – Joseph about their recent move to Colorado, and Alfred about his plans for the years to come.

"Was thinking of heading back east. Not sure I could find work out here, given my reputation."

Joseph smiled. "I might be able to help in that department."

Cadence stood motionless, letting the simple sounds of life fade to a muffled hum.

She wasn't hungry now. The hunger only came once over the years – one late night in an outpost on the road to Colorado. Joseph had chosen to remain as himself when they hunkered down for a night in a rented room. The landlord saw Joseph slip into Cadence's bedroom, and when morning came, the meddling bastard came after Joseph, threatening a noose. Cadence happily met the man in the quiet back room of his outpost and tore his heart out with her bare hands. Moments later, she appeared to the rest of the outpost as its newly late proprietor and demanded Joseph's release. Until that night, the last time she'd eaten the heart of a man was Matthew Clairmont, and even that heart was more out of spite than hunger.

Still, the powers Joseph had given her left her seemingly ageless, powerful, and as a result of time and well placed compulsion, very wealthy.

What better way to celebrate their wealth than to help the less fortunate, Joseph had said.

Cadence turned to watch Joseph and Alfred drink and laugh, smiling as Joseph danced around the subject of offering Alfred a job in one of their businesses in Littleton.

"You don't think you'd have trouble? You know, havin me around?"

"No, Al. You'll be welcome there. And if anyone gives you any trouble, you can just -"

Alfred raised a hand and shook his head. "Don't you say it. You know I ain't no mind to be telling anyone what to do."

Cadence crossed the room to stand at Joseph's shoulder, touching her hand to the hard shape of him. She wanted the warmth of him. She was growing tired, and the thought of his side of the bed being empty left her feeling cold.

He reached up and squeezed her hand. "Ah, yes. I forgot how you felt about that, friend. My apologies."

Cadence gave Alfred a kind smile, taking in the older man anew. He was worn in a way only prison could mark a man, but his eyes were friendly and hopeful. She'd heard Joseph speak of Alfred many times – of his gentleness and humor. Still, hearing Alfred spurn the mere notion of compelling another – of using the powers that Shannon Bell's heart gave him on that mountain in Colorado so many years ago – made her soften to him. Had he wanted to in the last two decades, he could have forced the guards of his prison to release him. Yet, he stayed, serving his time for a crime he didn't commit.

A sound startled her toward the stairs, a high pitch bleat that was so sudden, she almost believed she'd imagined it.

Joseph turned toward the stairs as well just as the sound returned, this time, sustained. Both Joseph and Alfred stood, but Cadence was already halfway up the stairs, her skirts billowing around her ankles.

The cry sounded again, powered now by a new draw of breath. She slipped into her bedroom and leaned over the tiny basinet to look into her daughter's frustrated face. Cadence leaned down to collect Maxine, her long nightgown twisted snugly around her chubby legs.

"Aw, might I have a look?" Alfred asked, his voice barely a whisper as Cadence descended the stairs with her beautiful daughter in her arms. Without a second thought, Cadence handed the tiny, black-haired girl to Alfred Packer and watched him slump down into a nearby chair, cooing into Maxine's tan face. She watched him for a long moment, wondering how anyone had ever though such a man capable of the dark deeds he was accused of.

She remembered the weeks she spent on the receiving end of that same suspicion and smiled.

However trying those days had been, they'd given her freedom.

"Momma? Is someone here?"

Joseph turned for the stairs and rushed to snatch up his son, carrying him down the rest of the way to meet Alfred. Young Percy looked exactly like his father – black hair, tanned skin, but unlike Joseph, Percy's eyes were blue – the one piece of Cadence in the otherwise native looking boy.

Joseph let the children meet Alfred, putting a blissful smile on the man's face before showing him to his room for the night and tucking Percy back into his bed.

Cadence settled Maxine into her crib and curled herself under the feather quilts of her bed. She sat there in the half light, watching Joseph slip out of his clothes and come to lie beside her. He left his hair braided as he settled his head on the pillow beside her.

They stared into each other's eyes, smiling for a long moment.

Cadence touched her hand to Joseph's cheek. "If you think it's time, I'm ready," she said.

Joseph sighed audibly, letting his forearm fall across his eyes. "Thank you," he whispered, turning to kiss her cheek, then her temple, and finally her lips.

Maxine cooed softly in her sleep across the room as Joseph slipped his arms around Cadence's middle.

"You still have it?" She asked.

Joseph pressed his face into her hair and nodded. "Yes. I visited Beatrice before we headed west."

She closed her eyes and fought with the notion of what they would do. Percy was almost twelve, and despite being a strong and patient young man, he'd grown up having to accept the common belief that he was adopted by two charitable white folks instead of the full blood son of a white woman and a native man that loved each other very much. They'd moved to Colorado to give him a new life, building a great house in the country where Percy could run and play, free from scrutiny in the bustling city of Cheyenne. Yet, even in the country, people stared or turned up their nose when he travelled into town with his mother or father.

Cadence was tired of watching her son suffer because of the ignorance of lesser men. She was tired of seeing him afraid to be her son.

Cadence took a deep breath, glancing across the room toward Maxine's crib. Maxine was still young, but Cadence dreaded her daughter feeling that same alienation when she grew old enough to understand.

It was time. She was ready to free Percy of that weight. She was ready for Percy to become like them.

"If he wants it, let him have it tomorrow. Then teach him what you taught me."

Joseph squeezed her so tight, she felt her joints crack. She thought back to that night so long ago – the last time she'd taken a life.

Percy had been the very reason the bastard in the outpost was so angry. He'd seen little Percy's black hair when Cadence held her then toddler to her chest. He'd assumed Joseph – the real, native man – was Percy's father. And how dare a native man father a child with a white woman?

It seemed only fitting that the bigot's heart, now salted and dried, packed away for just this possibility, would be the very thing to spare their beloved son from the bigotry of others.

Joseph would teach Percy how to live behind the outpost owner's face, appearing as the young boy the outposter had once been, growing through the years as the white man did, Percy only showing his true face when he chose to. Joseph would teach him how to move among the white folk unseen, and in the end, how to be free of the oppression of any other.

Whatever darkness she'd committed in murdering that man, she felt only light in the knowledge that it might free her son of scrutiny if he chose to avoid it.

Joseph pressed his arms up under her breasts and squeezed her against him. His breathing shifted, evidence of his falling asleep. Cadence lay there listening to their daughter's quiet snores and fell asleep in her husband's arms.

THE END

AFTERWORD

I apologize to anyone who lost their freaking mind when this book turned to cannibalism right out of the gate.

I just apologize.

I promise I won't do it again. At least, not right out of the gate.

-Michaela
XOXO

Actually...hang on.

I have been known to write Native characters in a good amount of my work. Under Michaela Carr, I have an entire family saga that takes place within a Native family. I sometimes don't even realize the characters or storylines are coming until they're already underway. That tendency is heavily influenced by my growing up with two Native older brothers. And good grief, was I blessed to have them.

The romanticized notion of the West was something I heard all about on those road trips with gram, but at home with my brothers, I heard the truth behind those stories. The history we're often taught about America is built on the stories of those who survived in this landscape. The West existed wholly due to the slaughter and oppression of Indigenous people, and then by the work of women. The men who thrived on this Stolen Land long enough to write history rarely gave credit where credit was due. Our history books often overlook our Indigenous people, creating heroes out of villains and folklore out of Native people's lived experiences. And rarely is the contribution of women ever acknowledged to its full merit.

Men. Amirite?

After all, the writers of history are usually those who could afford the pen and the time to write. Women were too busy working, and our Native communities were having their voices silenced.

I have contemplated rewriting this book to remove some of the liberties I've taken with Indigenous stories and beliefs. Yet, each time I refrain. This book is a reflection of the voices in my head at that time, and it's a quiet nod to the truth of the American Experience for many of our ancestors.

Cadence's ending is the truth of every 'pioneer.' The heroes of our stories – even those we root for, who we believe to have been the best of us – were fatally flawed. As are most of us.

The job is to try to be better. And I have to acknowledge that I can, and I hope to do better.

About Author

Michaela Wright is the author of the Gothic Romance Mystery series, The NAMESAKEN GOTHICS. Michaela spent years as a historical interpreter, and her regular stints in the countryside of Scotland helped to inspire her steamy love stories. Given her love of the haunting side of history, her writing has been known to keep readers up at night in more ways than one.

Michaela writes from Chelmsford, Massachusetts, where she lives with her family.

You can reach Michaela at

MichaelaWrightAuthor@gmail.com

ALSO BY

AND WRITING AS

Miranda Newfield

CATCH MY FALL

WRITING MR RIGHT

SHAKE OFF THE GHOSTS

And as *Michaela Carr*

SAVING HER BEAR

BEARLY BURNING

THE UNCHOSEN BRIDE

TRUE NORTH

THE WAY HOME

www.ingramcontent.com/pod-product-compliance
Lightning Source LLC
LaVergne TN
LVHW041158150826
845673LV00001B/207
* 9 7 8 1 5 3 9 9 8 5 2 7 3 *